ANDERSEN'S
FAIRY TALES

*There was a knocking at the gate of the town, and the
old King went to open it.*   (See page 137)

ANDERSEN'S FAIRY TALES

by Hans Christian Andersen

introduction by WILLIAM T. ATWOOD
illustrated by FREDERICK RICHARDSON
color illustrations by DONALD E. COOKE

HOLT, RINEHART and WINSTON, *New York*

Contents

List of Illustrations

Introduction

EVERY once in a while a man is born who is able to see the magic, the mystery, the poetry beneath the surface of familiar things. This ability we call imagination—the power to picture vividly the unseen. Some of these men see the lightning and turn electricity into the genii that light our homes, power our machines, and operate our telephones. Others, like Hans Christian Andersen, translate them into the delightful allegories we call fairy tales, and charm our minds with happy thoughts. Whether these mysterious forces are pictured as atoms or as fairies, the result is the same: the enrichment of our understanding.

We read Andersen's stories for enjoyment, but there is a subtle lesson in every one. The tale of Hans Clodhopper shows that those in high places are moved by the same impulses as everyone else. The princess is more impressed by Hans' ready wit than by the wisdom of his learned brothers. The Bell shows that the same objective may be attained in different ways and by proud and humble alike, and that the half-hearted never reach the heights. The Emperor's New Clothes satirizes fear of ridicule. So through all the tales runs an unobtrusive, but easily apparent, lesson. To paraphrase the Duchess in *Alice in Wonderland*, "Every one has a moral, if you can only find it." Even the longer and more complex stories like The Traveling Companion and The Marsh King's Daughter teach the reward of goodness and the defeat of evil.

Andersen writes in the simple unaffected style of a truly great storyteller. He relates his tale with the directness and lack of elaboration of a news item, yet so convincing is his sincerity that, however extravagant their acts, his characters are to the reader real beings doing nothing that is not natural. There is nothing incongruous in the wicked princess flying to the wizard's cave or in her invisible pursuer with swan's wings, so perfect is the illusion. This, indeed, is literary greatness.

Though it was probably not so intended, The Ugly Duckling is almost autobiographical of the author. Born in poverty and early orphaned, he was left to his own devices. Ungainly in person and of a dreamy disposition, his early youth was lonely and unhappy. His dreary hours were occupied in the construction of a puppet theater in which he produced the works of the great dramatists as well as his own efforts at play writing. But despite his apparent dullness, he was a keen observer of the people about him. His imagination saw through the obvious and endowed the homely affairs of life and the humdrum persons he met with the mystery and poetry that were later to make his fairy tales famous. Workaday citizens, touched by his wizardry, were to become kings and adventurers, the shopkeeper's daughter a princess; the storks on the chimney tops were to be transformed into fairy messengers; moles and field mice, larks and toads were to play parts in his stories; even the flax plant and the broken bottle were to tell their tales.

Andersen's flair for dramatics led him to attempt successively to become an opera singer and a dancer. He failed in both, and in Copenhagen, where he had gone to study these arts, he was regarded as little better than a lunatic. However a few influential friends, and later the King, saw possibilities in the imaginative youth and befriended him. Presently he began to write. Various stories and romances appeared, and some were successful. Then came the Fairy Tales, which were an immediate success. The Ugly Duckling had become the Swan. The author was feted by the rich and great; he was beloved by the people. Children and adults have from that day delighted in the many translations of his immortal book. Today a statue of Hans Christian Andersen, bought with pennies of school children, adorns a public square in Copenhagen.

—WILLIAM T. ATWOOD

The Snow Queen ᎒

Iɴ a large city lived a little boy named Kay and a little girl named Gerda. They played together in the summertime in the fields, and when the snow began to fly they got their sleds and went skimming down the hills. One day Kay took his sled down to the public square and was playing with the other boys when he noticed a large sleigh, painted all in white, and in it sat a figure muffled up in a shaggy white fur, with a cap on.

The sleigh drove ten times round the square, and Kay fastened his sled to it. It drove faster and faster, and then turned into one of the streets that ran out of the square. The snow began to fall thickly, and Kay thought he had better start back for home. He tried to unfasten his sled, but he found he could not get loose.

On they flew as fast as the wind, clean off the ground, and over the hedges. At last the big sleigh stopped, and the person driving it stood up, and Kay

now saw that it was a lady, tall and slim and dazzlingly white.

"I am the Snow Queen," she said. "Don't you
want to come and see what a beautiful place I live
in?" The little boy felt so cold he could make no
answer. So she came and lifted him out of his sled
and put him beside her and tucked the big fur robe
around him. Then off they went again.

It was a long, dreary winter for Gerda, who
missed her little playmate. One day in the spring,
when she was out in the woods, an old woman
came to her and said, "My child, come and you will
see the most beautiful garden in the world."

Gerda was fond of flowers, and she followed the
old woman, who led her through some winding
paths and at last brought her to the garden. Oh,
how sweet and beautiful! There were all kinds of
flowers of every season of the year, and Gerda
played here many days in the warm sunshine.

Before she knew it, winter had come again. One
day there came a raven, hopping over the snow.
"Caw! Caw!" said the raven. "If you knew what
I know you would be happy."

"Why, what do you know?" asked Gerda.

"I know where Kay is," said the raven.

And now Gerda's heart was all a-flutter. "Oh,
is he still alive? And will you tell me how I can
find him?"

"Yes," said the raven, "as soon as I have spoken with the robber girl." Gerda did not know what the raven meant by the "robber girl." But very soon she was to know, for in a few days, back came the raven perched on the shoulder of a strong-looking girl.

"I am the robber girl," she said. "I live here in the woods, and the menfolk go out and take the treasures of rich men; but we are kind to poor folk. The raven has told me about your little friend Kay, and I have come to take you to him."

So away went Gerda with the robber girl, who led her to where a reindeer was standing. She lifted Gerda on to its back, put cushions and robes around her, and then said, "Now go, reindeer, away to the Snow Queen's kingdom where this little girl's playmate is. Take good care of her."

Then the reindeer, with Gerda on its back, bounded away, over the hedges and fields, faster and faster. Away up in frozen Lapland the door of a little hut built right in the snow opened, and an old woman came out to give them food and drink. Then away they went again.

At last the reindeer stopped. "We are just outside the Snow Queen's palace," it said. "I cannot go in. But you may enter. Go straight on over the ice and you will see your playmate. You will find him cold, for he has become one of the Snow

Queen's family, and they are all frozen to the heart.
If you sing a hymn or weep hard enough you may
break the spell. I will wait here, but do not linger,
for I must hurry back."

Gerda felt as if she were almost frozen herself,
and when she looked all about her there was
nothing but great icebergs, and away in the distance
something that looked like a palace of diamonds.
But she went on and on and on, and coming close
to the great palace, which she now saw was an ice
palace, she caught sight of Kay, standing all alone.

She ran over the ice to him as fast as she could,
and put her arms around him. "Kay! Dear little
Kay!" she cried. "I have found you at last!"

But he stood quite still, stiff and cold, and little
Gerda cried bitter, burning tears. But she thought
she saw a flush begin to come into his frozen
cheeks, and then, remembering what the reindeer
had said, she began to sing:

"The rose blooms, but its glory past,
Christmas then comes so fast."

And, like magic, new life came into the cold body
of Kay, and when he saw his little playmate he
cried out in delight, "Gerda! Is it really you,
little Gerda? Where have you been all this time?
and where——"

Then the reindeer, with Gerda on its back, bounded away.

But Gerda did not stop to answer his questions. "We must hurry," she said. "The reindeer will think we aren't coming."

She caught his arm and quickly led him out of the Snow Queen's domain. In a few moments they were on the back of the reindeer, hurrying back over the fields of snow and ice. Nor did the reindeer stop till it reached the city where Gerda and Kay lived.

Kay and Gerda are married now and have children of their own. And of all the stories the children love to hear, they like best the one about the Snow Queen.

The Steadfast Tin Soldier

T HERE were once five and twenty tin soldiers who were brothers, for they had all been made from the same old tin spoon. They were very grand in their new red and blue uniforms, as they shouldered their guns and looked straight before them.

The first thing the soldiers ever heard were the words, "Tin Soldiers!" shouted by a little boy, who clapped his hands with delight when the lid was taken off the box in which they lived.

It was the little boy's birthday, and the soldiers had been given to him for a birthday present. The little boy took the soldiers out of the box and stood them on the table. They were exactly alike, except one, who had only one leg. He was the last one to be made, and there had not been enough tin to finish him; but he stood as firmly on one leg as the others did on two.

There were many other playthings on the table where the soldiers stood; but the most attractive one

was a pretty little paper castle. The windows were
very tiny, but still one could look through them and
see the inside of the rooms. In front of the castle
stood little trees around a piece of looking-glass, which
looked like a lake of clear water. Beautiful little wax
swans were swimming about the lake and were reflected on its glassy surface.

This was all very pretty; but the prettiest thing
of all was a tiny little lady, who stood at the open
door of the castle. She also was made of paper;
but her dress was of the thinnest muslin, with a
narrow blue ribbon like a scarf over her shoulders.
At the middle of the ribbon was a shining tinsel
rose as big as her whole face.

The little lady stretched out both her arms, for she
was a dancer, and she raised one foot so high that the
tin soldier could not see it at all, and thought that she
also had but one leg.

"She would make a fine wife for me," said the
soldier; "only she is so grand and lives in a castle,
while I have only a box to live in. Besides, there
are five and twenty of us in the box, and there is
no room for her. Still I must try to become ac-
quainted with her."

Then he lay down at full length behind the snuffbox, where he could watch the dainty little lady,
who still stood on one leg without losing her bal-
ance.

When evening came, the tin soldiers were put into the box—that is, all of them except the soldier with one leg, who was left standing on the table—and the people of the house went to bed. Then the toys began to play and have jolly times on the table. The tin soldiers rattled in their box, for they wanted to get out and play with the others; but they could not lift the lid. The nutcracker turned somersaults, and the pencil jumped about the table. They made so much noise that the canary woke up and began to sing in the middle of the night. Only the tin soldier and the dancer remained in their places. She stretched out both her arms and stood on tiptoe as firmly as he did on his one leg. He never turned his eyes from her, even for a single moment.

The clock struck twelve. Up flew the lid of the snuffbox, but there was no snuff in it; for it was not a real snuffbox, but only the house of a goblin named Jack-in-the-Box.

The goblin looked very fierce and said, "Tin soldier, keep your eyes to yourself."

The tin soldier pretended not to hear him, and that made the goblin very angry. He snapped his teeth and said, "Only wait till tomorrow! Then you'll see!"

The next morning the children put the tin soldier in the window. No one knows whether it was the

goblin or the wind that did it, but it is certain that
the soldier fell from the third-story window to the
street below. It was a terrible fall. He landed
on his head, and his bayonet wedged in between
some stones and held him there with his one leg
straight up in the air.

The maid and the little boy went downstairs to
look for him; but, although they nearly stepped
upon him, they could not find him. If the soldier
had called out, "Here I am!" they would have
found him; but he did not care to call for help
because he was a soldier.

Then it began to rain. The drops fell faster and
faster until there was a regular shower. When the
shower was over, two boys who were idling about
the street happened to pass by.

"Look," said one of them, "here is a tin soldier.
He ought to have a boat to sit in."

So they made a boat from a newspaper, and
stood the tin soldier in it and sent him sailing down
the gutter. Then the two boys ran along beside
him, clapping their hands. The waves were very
high and the current was strong. The paper boat
rocked up and down, and it sometimes turned
so quickly that the soldier trembled; but he stayed
at his post. He shouldered his musket and looked
straight before him.

All at once, the boat shot into a long drain,

where it was as dark as it was in the box where the other tin soldiers lived.

"Where am I going now?" thought he. "This must surely be the goblin's fault. Oh! if only the little lady were here with me in the boat, I should not care how dark it was."

A huge water rat that lived under the bridge soon came in sight.

"Have you a pass?" asked the rat; but the tin soldier kept silent and held his musket tighter than ever.

The boat flew past, and the rat followed. How he gnashed his teeth and called out to the wood shavings and the straw. "Stop him! stop him! he has not paid his toll or shown his pass."

The stream carried the tin soldier on more rapidly than ever, and he could already see daylight where the drain ended. Then he heard a rushing sound that was enough to frighten the bravest man. At the end of the drain the water fell into a canal; this was as dangerous for his tiny craft as going over a waterfall would be for a boat.

The little paper boat dashed on, but the soldier stood as firmly as he could, to show that he was not afraid. The boat whirled around three or four times until it was filled with water. Then it began to sink. The tin soldier stood up to his neck in water, while the boat sank deeper and deeper.

Soon the water closed over his head. He thought of the pretty little dancer whom he should never see again, and he was very sad.

Then the paper boat became soft and was torn to pieces. The soldier dropped down deeper into the water, but was at once swallowed by a huge fish.

Oh, how dark it was inside the fish! It was even darker than it was in the drain, and there was no room for him to move; but the tin soldier kept his courage and lay at full length with his gun on his shoulder.

The fish swam about, making the most fearful movements, but at last it became quite still. Then a flash of lightning seemed to dart through him. Daylight appeared, and a voice called out, "As I am alive, the tin soldier!" The fish had been caught, taken to the market, and sold to the cook, who took him to the kitchen and cut him open with a large knife. She picked up the soldier, held him by the waist between her thumb and finger, and carried him into another room where everybody was surprised to see this wonderful soldier who had traveled about inside a fish. But he was not at all proud.

They put him on the table. What curious things happen in the world! The soldier was in the very same room in which he had been before. He saw the same children, and the same toys stood on the table; and there was the same castle with the pretty little dancer. She was still standing on one foot and holding up the other. She was as firm and as faithful as he was. He was almost moved to tears. He looked longingly at her and she looked at him; but they said nothing.

Then one of the little boys took up the tin soldier and threw him into the stove. He gave no reason for doing this, so it must have been the fault of the goblin.

The flames gathered around him and the heat was terrible; but he could not tell whether the heat came from the fire or from love. His bright red and blue colors were gone, but whether that had happened on his travels or had been caused by sorrow, no one could say. He looked at the little lady and she looked at him. He felt himself melting away, but still he stood there with his gun on his shoulder.

Suddenly the door of the room opened, and the wind caught up the dancer and whirled her right into the stove beside the tin soldier. Instantly, she was caught up by the flames and was gone. The tin soldier melted down to a lump, and the next morning when the maid took out the ashes, she found him in the shape of a little tin heart. Nothing remained of the dancer but the tinsel rose, and that was burned as black as a coal.

The Wild Swans ❧

THERE once lived a king who had eleven sons, and a beautiful daughter named Eliza. The eleven princes and the Princess Eliza were very happy till their mother died. Then the king married a wicked woman who turned the eleven boys into wild swans.

Eliza did not know what had become of them, and she wandered about, very sad of heart. One day when she was on a little hill overlooking the ocean she saw eleven swans flying toward her over the sea. Just as the sun went down they dropped to the ground beside her. Their feathers fell off, and behold, there stood her eleven brothers!

"Oh, now we can always be together," cried Eliza.

But the oldest brother shook his head. "No," he said. "Our wicked stepmother has bewitched us, and we must stay swans as long as the sun shines.

14

But every night, at sundown, we become men again. We do not live here, but far over the sea."

"Take me with you," pleaded the princess. So they made a great net of young willows and rushes. When morning came, and they had become swans again, they took the net with their beaks and carried the girl away over the sea.

Toward evening a fearful storm arose, with lightning and thunder but just before sundown they reached a rock, and the brothers became men again. The lightning still flashed from the heavens, but the Princess Eliza was not afraid, for her brothers joined hands around the rock, and she felt quite safe.

Next morning her swan brothers carried her off to a beautiful country, and there she fell fast asleep. She dreamed that a fairy came to her and told her that she could break the spell if she made shirts of nettles and threw them over the swans. But she must not speak all the time she was at work.

When she awoke she remembered her dream and set to work. The nettles stung her poor hands, but she did not stop for that.

When her brothers came that night they saw her hands all blistered and asked her what had happened. But she said nothing.

The next day the king of that country caught

sight of Eliza, and he fell in love with her at once and asked her to marry him. Eliza looked up into his kind face, but she said nothing.

The king pitied her, for he thought she was dumb. Then he took her away to his palace and there was a splendid wedding. But Eliza was not happy. She wandered into the woods and gathered nettles and worked upon the shirts.

Then some of the people said she was a witch. But she worked on till she had ten shirts finished and the eleventh almost completed. In those days the people believed in witches, and it was not long till they cried out that the girl must die, so they carried her out and were just about to tie her to a post when eleven wild swans dropped down beside her. All the people were frightened. Eliza broke through them, and catching up the eleven shirts, she threw them over the swans; and behold, her dear brothers stood beside her.

"Tell the king I can speak now," cried Eliza; and when he had come she told the story of why she had been silent so long. Then all the people praised her, and the king gave a great dinner party for her and the eleven princes, who were never to be swans again.

The Swineherd ❧

THERE was once a Prince who was poor, for his kingdom was very small, but still it was large enough for him to think of getting married, and think of it he did.

It was certainly rather bold of him that he dared to say to the Emperor's daughter, "Will you have me?" But he dared for all that, for his name was famous far and near, and there were hundreds of Princesses who would readily have said "Yes"; but did she say so?

Now we shall hear.

On the grave of the Prince's father there grew a rose tree—oh, such a beautiful rose tree—for, though it blossomed only every fifth year and then bore but one rose, that was a rose with such a delicious scent that whoever smelt it forgot all care and trouble. He also had a nightingale, which sang as if all the most beautiful melodies lived together in its little throat.

This rose and this nightingale the Princess was to have, and so they were put in silver boxes and sent to her.

The Emperor had them carried before him into the great hall, where the Princess was playing at "puss in the corner" with her ladies-in-waiting, and when she saw the large boxes with the presents she clapped her hands with delight.

"I hope it's a little kitten," she said; but there was the rose tree with the beautiful rose.

"Oh, how pretty it is done!" all the ladies cried.

"It is more than pretty, it is beautiful," the Emperor said.

"Faugh, papa!" the Princess cried, "it is not artificial, it is natural."

"Faugh!" all the ladies cried, "it is natural."

"Let us first see what is in the other box before we grow angry," the Emperor said; and then the nightingale came out, singing so beautifully that nothing could be said against it.

"*Superbe, charmant!*" all the ladies cried, for they all jabbered French, one worse than the other.

"How the bird reminds me of the musical box of the late Empress," an old courtier said. "It is exactly the same tone—the same tune."

"Yes," the Emperor said, and he cried like a little child.

"I hope that at least is not natural," the Princess said.

"Yes, it is a natural bird," those who brought it answered.

"Then let the bird fly," the Princess said; and she would by no means let the poor Prince come.

But he came for all that. He painted his face with brown and black, pulled his cap down over his eyes, and knocked at the gate.

"Good day, Emperor," he said. "Can I get some work here in the palace?"

"Yes, certainly," the Emperor answered. "I want someone to look after the pigs, for we have a great many."

So the Prince was appointed imperial swineherd. He had a miserable little room down near the pigsty, and there he had to live; but the whole day he sat working, and when night came he had made a pretty little iron pot, with bells all round, and as soon as the pot boiled they rang so prettily, and played the old tune, "Home, Sweet Home." But the most curious part was, that by holding one's finger in the steam of the boiling pot, one could at once smell what food was being prepared in every house in the town. Now, that was a very different thing from the rose.

The next time the Princess went out with her ladies she heard the beautiful melody and was quite delighted, for she too could play "Home, Sweet Home," —it was the only thing she could play, and that she played with one finger.

"That is the very same tune that I play," she said; "and he must be a very skilful swineherd. One of you go down and ask him the price of the instrument."

So one of the ladies had to go down, but she put on wooden clogs.

"What do you want for the iron pot?" the lady asked.

"I must have ten kisses from the Princess," the swineherd answered.

"Heaven forbid!" the lady cried.

"I cannot take less," he replied.

"He is a rude fellow," the Princess said, and she went on, but had not gone many steps when the bells sounded so prettily, "Home, Sweet Home."

"Go again, and ask him whether ten kisses from my ladies will not do."

"I am very much obliged," he answered, "they must be ten kisses from the Princess herself, or I keep my instrument."

"What rubbish all this is!" the Princess said. "Now you must all stand round me, so that no one may see it."

Then the ladies stood round her, spreading out their dresses and the swineherd got the ten kisses, and the Princess the iron pot.

Never did anything give so much pleasure. The whole evening, and the whole of the following day, the iron pot had to keep boiling, so that there was

The next time the Princess went out with her ladies she heard the beautiful melody.

not a single hearth in the whole town that they did not know what had been cooked on it—at the Prime Minister's as well as at the shoemaker's. The ladies danced about, clapping their hands.

"We know who will have sweet soup and omelets for dinner, and who will have broth and sausages. Oh, how interesting that is!"

"Yes; but you must not blab, for I am the Emperor's daughter."

"The Lord forbid!" all cried.

The swineherd, that is, the Prince—but no one knew he was anything more than a real swineherd— did not pass his time idly. He had now made a rattle which, when swung round, played all the waltzes and quadrilles that had been heard from the beginning of the world.

"Oh, that is superb!" the Princess said as she passed. "I have never heard a more beautiful piece of music. Go and ask him how much the instrument costs; but I will not kiss again."

"He asks a hundred kisses from the Princess," the lady said who went in to ask.

"I believe he is mad," the Princess said, and she went on, but had not got many yards when she stopped. "We must encourage artists," she said; "and

One day when she was on a little hill overlooking the ocean, She saw eleven swans flying toward her ...

am I not the Emperor's daughter? Go and tell him that he shall have ten kisses from me the same as the last time, and the rest he can have from my ladies."

"Oh, but we are very unwilling!" the ladies cried.

"What rubbish that is!" the Princess said. "When I can kiss him I should think you can, too; and remember that I feed you and pay you wages."

So what could they do but go again?

"A hundred kisses from the Princess," he said, "or let each keep his own."

"Stand there," she said. The ladies stood round her, and the kissing began.

"What is all that noise at the pigsty?" the Emperor cried, as he stepped out on the balcony. He rubbed his eyes, and put on his spectacles. "Why, it is the court ladies, who are up to some of their tricks! I suppose I must go and look after them." So he pulled his slippers up at the heel, for they were shoes the heels of which he had trodden down.

What haste he did make to be sure!

When he reached the yard he walked quite softly, and the ladies were so busily engaged counting the kisses, to make sure all was fair, that they did not notice him. He stood on tiptoe.

"What's this?" he cried, when he saw them kissing, and he hit them on the head with his slipper, just as the swineherd was receiving the eighty-sixth kiss.

"Get out with you!" he said, for he was very angry; and the Princess, as well as the swineherd, was sent away from the empire.

There she now stood, crying; the swineherd grumbled and the rain came pouring down.

"Oh, miserable wretch!" the Princess cried. "If I had only taken the handsome Prince! Oh dear, how unhappy I am!"

The swineherd now went behind a tree, washed the black and brown from his face, threw off the shabby clothes, and came in his Prince's costume, so handsome that the Princess curtsied to him.

"I only despise you now," he said. "You would not have an honest Prince, and you did not know how lovely were the rose and the nightingale, but were ready enough to kiss the swineherd just to get a plaything. Now you see what you get for it all."

He then went into his kingdom, and shut the door in her face. Now she could sing, "Home, Sweet Home."

The Little Mermaid ✑

FAR out at sea the water is as blue as the loveliest cornflower and as clear as the purest crystal. But it is very deep—deeper than anchor ever yet reached; many church towers would have to be piled one upon the other to reach right up from the bottom to the surface. Down there live the Seafolk.

The most wondrous trees and plants grow there, the stalks and leaves are so easily bent that they wave to and fro at the least motion of the water, just as if they were living beings. All the fishes, small and great, glide among the branches just as the birds fly about the trees up here. In the deepest spot of all lies the Sea-King's palace. The walls are of coral and the tall, pointed windows of the clearest amber, while the roof is of shells, which open and shut according to the tide; and lovely they look, for in every one of the shells lies a glistening pearl, any of which would be the glory of a queen's crown.

The Sea-King's wife had been dead for many years,

so his old mother kept house for him. She was a wise woman and very proud. She always went about with twelve oysters on her tail, the other important folk being allowed to wear only six. Yet she was very well thought of, especially because of the loving care she took of the little sea-princesses, her granddaughters. They were six pretty children, but the youngest was the loveliest of them all. Her skin was as delicately tinted as a rose leaf, and her eyes were as blue as the deepest sea, but, like all the others, she had no feet, her body ending in a fish's tail.

All day they used to play in the great rooms of the palace, where living flowers grew upon the walls. When the large amber windows were opened the fishes would swim through them just as the swallows fly into our houses when we open the windows; only the fishes swam right up to the little princesses, ate out of their hands, and let themselves be patted.

Around the palace was a large garden full of bright red and dark blue trees; the fruit shone like gold, and the flowers like burning fire, as the stalks and leaves moved to and fro. The soil itself was the finest sand, but blue as sulphur flames. A wonderful blue tint lay over everything; one would think that one was high up in the air with nothing but sky above and below rather than at the bottom of the sea. During a calm, too, one could catch a glimpse of the sun; it looked like a crimson flower, from whose cup light streamed out.

Each of the little princesses had her own garden-plot where she could dig and plant as she pleased. One gave her flower-plot the form of a whale; another wished hers to look like a little mermaid; but the youngest planted hers in a circle to look like the sun and would only have flowers which shone red like it. She was a strange child, silent and thoughtful, and while her sisters delighted to make their gardens pretty with all the strangest things they could get from wrecked vessels, all that she would have, besides the rosy-red flowers which looked like the sun, was a pretty statue of a handsome boy, cut out of pure white marble, which had sunk to the bottom of the sea during a shipwreck. She planted by this statue a rosy-red weeping willow; it grew splendidly and its fresh branches hung over the statue, nearly down to the sandy bottom where the shadows took a violet tint and moved to and fro like the branches. It seemed as if the top of the tree were at play with its roots, each trying to snatch kisses.

The little mermaid's greatest joy was to hear about the world of men above. She made her old grandmother tell her all she knew about ships and towns, people and animals. What she thought specially wonderful was that the flowers which grew upon the

earth should give out sweet smells, which they did
not do at the bottom of the sea; and that the woods
were green; and that the *fishes* among the branches
could sing so loudly and beautifully that it was a joy
to listen to them. It was the little birds that her
grandmother called *fishes*; the little girls would not
have understood her if she had called them *birds*.

"When you are fifteen," said the grandmother, "you
shall be allowed to swim up out of the sea and sit in
the moonshine on the rocks and see the big ships sail
by; you shall see woods and cities too."

In the following year one of the sisters would be
fifteen years old, but how about the others? Each was
a year younger than the one before, so the youngest
would have to wait five whole years before it would
be her turn to come up from the bottom of the sea
and see what our world is like. But each promised
to tell the others what she had seen and what she had
thought the most remarkable on the first day; for their
grandmother did not tell them half enough, and there
were many things they wanted to know about.

But none of them wished so much to go as the
youngest, just the one who had the longest to wait and
was so silent and thoughtful. Many a time she stood
at the open window and looked up through the dark
blue water where the fishes dashed about with their
fins and tails. She could see the moon and stars; of
course, they shone quite faintly, but at the same time

they looked twice as large through the water as they look to us. When something like a dark cloud glided across, she knew that it was either a whale swimming overhead, or else a ship with many people on board, who certainly never dreamed that a pretty little mermaid stood below and stretched her white arms up toward the keel of their vessel.

And now the oldest princess was fifteen years old and might rise to the surface of the sea. When she came back she had hundreds of things to tell about, but the nicest of all, she said, was to lie in the moonshine on a sandbank in the calm sea, and to see close by the shore the large town where the lights were twinkling, like hundreds of stars, to hear the music and the noise and bustle of carts and men, to look at the many church towers and spires, and to hear the bells ringing. It was just because she could not go ashore that she longed so for all these things.

Oh, how the youngest sister listened. And afterwards, when she stood in the evening at the open window and looked up through the dark blue water, she thought of the great city with all its noise and bustle, and even fancied she heard the church bells ringing.

The next year the second sister had leave to mount up through the water and swim where she pleased. She rose just as the sun was going down and she thought the sunset the prettiest sight of all. The whole sky looked like gold, she said, and the beauty of the clouds was lovely. Red and violet, they had sailed right over her; but far quicker than they, a flock of wild swans had flown, like a long white veil, right over the place where the sun stood. She also swam towards the sun, but it sank, and the rosy gleam left behind was soon swallowed up by the sea and the clouds.

A year after that the third sister came up to the surface. She was the boldest of them all, so she swam up a broad river which ran into the sea. She saw pretty green hills covered with vines; castles and country houses peeped forth from lovely woods; she heard the birds singing, and the sun shone so that often she had to duck down under the water to cool her burning face. In a little creek she came upon a whole swarm of children; they were running about quite naked and splashing in the water. She wanted to play with them, but they ran away in terror, and a little black beast came up. It was a dog, but she had never seen a dog before; it barked so savagely at her that she was frightened and swam back to the open sea again. But never could she forget the lovely woods, the green hills and the pretty children who could swim in the water although they had no fishes' tails.

The fourth sister was not so bold. She stayed out in the middle of the sea and said that was nicest of all; for you could see for miles and miles around, and the sky above looked like a great glass bell. Ships she had seen too, but so far away they looked like sea-gulls; the merry dolphins had turned somersaults and the great whales had squirted water up through their nostrils, so that it seemed as if hundreds of fountains were playing all around.

And now came the turn of the fifth sister. Her birthday was in the winter, and she saw what the others had not seen the first time they went up. The sea had quite a green color and round about floated huge icebergs; each looked like a pearl, she said, and yet was far larger than the church towers which men had built. They had the strangest shapes and glittered like diamonds. She had placed herself on one of the largest, and all the vessels had hurried past in terror while she sat there and let the wind flutter her long, streaming hair; but towards evening the sky became cloudy, it thundered and lightened, while the dark sea lifted the large icebergs high up so that they shone in the strong glare of the lightning. All the ships took in their sails; everyone was afraid, but she sat calmly on her iceberg and watched the lightning as it zig-zagged into the troubled sea.

The first time each of the sisters rose to the surface of the water she was delighted with the new and beautiful things she saw, but afterwards, when they were grown-up girls and could go above whenever they chose, they did not care enough to take the trouble. They liked the deep water better.

Very often in the evenings the five sisters would entwine their arms and rise in a row to the surface of the water. They had beautiful voices, sweeter than any of ours, and when a gale was blowing and they feared that a ship might be lost, they would swim before the vessel and sing sweetly of how happy it was at the bottom of the sea, and tell the sailors not to be afraid to come down. But the sailors could not understand their words.

Now when her sisters thus rose arm in arm through the sea, the little sister would stay below alone looking up after them, and she felt as if she must cry; but mermaids have no tears, and so they suffer all the more.

"Oh, if only I were fifteen!" said she. "I know that I shall love the world above and the people who live there."

And at last she *was* fifteen years old.

"Well, now," said her grandmother, "come here and let me dress you like your sisters." And she placed a wreath of white lilies in her hair, but every petal was the half of a pearl, and the old lady told eight large oysters to cling fast to the Princess's train to show that she was a princess.

"But they hurt me so!" said the little mermaid.

"Yes, but one must suffer a little for appearances," said the old lady.

Oh, how gladly the little mermaid would have torn off all this finery and laid aside her wreath; the red flowers from her garden suited her much better; but she dared not do it. "Good-by!" she said gladly

and rose, light and bright as a bubble, up to the surface
of the water.

The sun had just sunk as she raised her head above
the sea, but the clouds were still pink and gold, and
in the midst of the pale sky sparkled the evening star,
so clear and lovely. The air was mild and cool and
the sea as still as a mirror.

A large black ship with three masts lay upon it;
only a single sail was up, for not a breath of wind
stirred and the sailors were sprawling about on the
masts and rigging. There was music and singing, and
as the evening darkened hundreds of gay-colored
lamps were lit, looking as if the flags of all nations
were waving in the air. The little mermaid swam
close up to the cabin window, and every time the
water lifted her she would peep in through the panes
and could see many finely-dressed people. The hand-
somest was the young Prince with his large black eyes.
He could not be more than sixteen years old, and this
was his birthday and that was why they were having
all this merriment. The sailors danced upon the deck,
and when the young Prince stepped up, more than a
hundred rockets rose into the air; they shone as bright
as day, so that the little mermaid was frightened and
dived down beneath the water. But she soon popped
up her head again and then it seemed as if all the stars
of heaven were falling down upon her. Never had
she seen such fireworks; large suns spun round and

round, throwing out sparks, splendid fiery fishes dashed about in the blue air, and everything was reflected in the clear, calm sea. On the ship itself it was so light that you could clearly see every rope and spar and every person. And oh! how handsome the young Prince looked, as he pressed people's hands and laughed and smiled while the music resounded through the lovely night.

It grew late, but the little mermaid could not take her eyes from the ship and the handsome Prince. The many-colored lanterns were put out; no more rockets rose into the air, and no more salutes were fired; but from deep down in the sea there came a murmuring and a roaring. Still she sat upon the water, rocking up and down with it so that she could look into the cabin. But now the ship took a swifter course; one sail after another was taken in; the billows rolled higher and there came lightning from far away.

A frightful storm was coming on; that was why the sailors reefed the sails. The huge ship pitched to and fro as it flew across the raging ocean; the water rose like great black mountains, but the ship dived like a swan between the billows and then rose again on their towering tops. The little mermaid thought this grand sport, but not so the sailors. The ship strained and cracked, the thick planks bent under the repeated shocks of the sea, the mast snapped in the middle, and the ship tipped over on her side while the water rushed into the hold. And now the little mermaid saw that they were in danger. For a moment it was so pitch dark that she could see nothing at all, but when a flash of lightning came it was bright enough for her to see everything on the ship. People were being tossed helplessly about. She looked especially for the young Prince and as the ship went to pieces, saw him sink into the sea. She was quite pleased, for now he would come down to her. But then she remembered that people cannot live under the water and that he would be dead by the time he reached her father's palace. Die he must not, oh no! So she swam among the spars and planks which drifted on the sea, quite forgetting that they might crush her. Then she ducked beneath the water, and rising again on the billows managed at last to reach the young Prince, who by now was scarcely able to swim any longer in the raging sea. His arms and legs began to fail him, his beautiful eyes were closed, he must surely have died if the little mermaid had not come to his help, holding his head above the water as the billows broke over them.

When morning dawned the storm passed, but not a fragment of the ship was to be seen. The sun rose red and beaming from the water; the Prince's cheeks regained the color of life, but his eyes were closed. The mermaid kissed his forehead and stroked back his wet hair. He looked just like the marble statue down in her little garden; she kissed him again and wished that he might live.

And now she saw in front of her the mainland, with

high blue mountains, on the tops of which the snow shone as though great flocks of white swans lay there. Near the shore were lovely green forests and in front stood a church. Lemon and orange trees grew in the garden, and in front of the gate stood tall palm trees. The sea formed a little creek here, quite calm but very deep, right up to the cliff where the sea had washed up the fine white sand; here she swam with the Prince and laid him on the sand, taking great care that his head should lie higher than his body in the warm sunshine.

And now the bells in the large white building started ringing, and a number of girls came walking through the garden. The little mermaid swam farther out behind some lofty rocks which rose out of the water, covering her hair and breast with sea-foam so that no one could see her face. There she watched to see who would come to the poor Prince.

It was not long before a young girl came that way; she was quite frightened when she saw him, but only for a moment. Then she brought a number of people, and the mermaid saw that the Prince came to life again, and smiled on those around him. But he did not send a smile to her, for, of course, he did not know that she had saved him. She felt so grieved that when he was carried away into the large building she dived down under the water, full of sorrow, and sought her father's palace.

She had always been silent and thoughtful, but after this she became still more so. Her sisters asked what she had seen when she went above for the first time, but she would tell them nothing.

Many a morning and many an evening she rose to the spot where she had last seen the Prince. She saw how the fruits of the garden ripened and were plucked; she saw how the snow melted on the lofty mountains, but the Prince she did not see, and every time she returned home more and more sorrowful. The only time she was happy was when she sat in her little garden and flung her arms around the pretty marble statue which was so like the Prince. But she did not attend to her flowers at all; they grew as if they were wild right over the paths and wreathed their long stalks and leaves among the branches of the trees till it was quite gloomy under their shade.

At last she told her story to one of her sisters, and so all the others learned of it; and then it reached the ears of two other mermaids, who told it to nobody but their closest friends. One of these happened to know who the Prince was and all about him; she also had seen the merrymaking on board the ship and knew where he came from and where his kingdom was.

"Come, little sister!" said the other Princesses, and with their arms around each other's shoulders, they rose in a long row out of the sea in the place where they knew the Prince's palace stood. This was built of a light yellow glistening stone, with broad marble staircases, one of which reached straight down to the sea. Through the high windows you looked into lovely rooms hung with rich silk curtains and large pictures, so that it was a pleasure to look at them.

So now she knew where the Prince lived, and many an evening and many a night she rose upon the water. She swam much nearer to the land than any of the others had dared to do; she even went up the narrow canal, under the marble balcony which cast a long shadow across the water. Here she used to sit and look at the young Prince, who fancied he was quite alone in the bright moonlight.

Many an evening she saw him sail in his splendid boat with banners waving and music playing; she would peep from among the green rushes, and when the wind played with her long silvery white veil and people caught sight of it, they took it to be a swan spreading its wings.

Many a night, too, when the fishermen were trailing their nets by torchlight, she heard them speaking of the young Prince and praising him so highly that she was more than ever glad that she had saved his life when he was drifting on the waves. And she remembered how his head had rested on her breast, and how she had kissed him; but as he knew nothing of all this, he could not even dream about her.

There was much she would have liked to know, but her sisters were not able to answer her questions.

So she asked her old grandmother who knew all about the upper world.

"If men do not get drowned," asked the little mermaid, "can they live forever? Don't they die as we do down here in the sea?"

"Yes," said the old dame, "they must die; and indeed their life is shorter than ours. We can live to be three hundred years old, but at last we become mere foam upon the water, and are not even buried among our dear ones. We have no souls; we never enter upon a new life; we are like the green rushes, if once they be cut down, they cannot grow again. But men have souls which always live—even after the body has been buried in the earth; they rise up through the clear air to the shining stars. Just as we rise out of the sea up to the lands of men, so their souls mount to beautiful regions which we shall never see."

"Why have we not souls?" asked the little mermaid sorrowfully. "I would give all the hundreds of years I may have to live to be a living child among men but for a single day so that I might hope to live in the world above the sky!"

"You must not bother your head about that," said the old grandmother. "We are much better and happier down here."

"So I shall die and float away like foam upon the sea, hear no more the music of the waves, and see no more the pretty flowers and the red sun! Can I then do nothing at all to win a soul?"

"There is only one way," said the old grandmother. "If a man grew to love you so dearly that you were more to him than father or mother, if he clung to you with all his heart and soul, and let the priest lay his right hand in yours and promised to be true to you here and always, then his soul would flow over to your body and you would have a share in the happiness of men. He would have given you a soul, and yet have kept his own. But that can never be! The very thing that is so pretty in the sea, here, your fish's tail, they think is hideous on earth, because they know no better. Up there one must have a couple of awkward things called legs to be thought handsome!"

Then the little mermaid sighed and looked sorrowfully at her fish's tail.

"Let us be contented," said the old grandmother, "and hop and skip about to our hearts' content in the three hundred years we have to live. Upon my word we have a nice long time of it. We'll have a Court ball this very evening!"

It was indeed a happy sight, such as one never sees on earth. The walls and ceiling of the vast dancing hall were of glass, thick but clear. Many hundreds of huge shells, rosy red and grassy green, were hung in rows on each side, full of blue blazing flames which lit up the whole room and shone right through the walls, so that the sea around was bright for a long distance. Countless fishes, small and

great, came swimming past the glass walls; the scales
of some of them shining purple red, while others
sparkled like gold and silver.

Through the great ballroom flowed a broad
stream, and on this the mermen and the mermaids
danced to their own pretty songs. Such lovely
voices are unknown on earth. The little mermaid
sang the sweetest of them all and they clapped their
hands with pleasure; for a moment her heart was
glad, for she knew that she had the loveliest voice
of all creatures on the earth or in the sea. But soon
her thoughts turned once more to the world above
her; she could not forget either the handsome Prince
or her sorrow at not having like him, a soul. So
soon she stole from her father's palace, with its mirth
and melody, and sat sorrowfully in her little garden.

Here she heard a bugle sounding down through
the water and she thought, "Now I know he is sailing
up above there—he whom I love more than my
father or mother, to whom the thoughts of my heart
cling and in whose hands I would willingly lay my
life's happiness. While my sisters are dancing in my
father's palace, I will go to the sea witch; I have
always before been afraid of her, but perhaps she
may help me."

So the little mermaid went right out of her own
part of the sea towards a whirlpool behind which
the sea witch lived. She had never gone that way

before. No flowers nor sea grasses grew there; only the bare gray sandy bottom stretched out toward the whirlpool where the water, like a rushing millstream, eddied round and round, dragging everything it caught into the deep. She had to go right through these to get to the sea witch's home. Beyond them stood her house in the midst of a most strange wood. All the trees and bushes were half animal, half vegetable, they looked like hundred-headed snakes growing out of the ground; all their branches were long slimy arms, with fingers like supple snakes, and they were twisting and twirling from the roots through every joint to the outermost tips of their branches. Everything in the sea which they could catch hold of they wound themselves about and never let go again. The little mermaid was quite frightened and stood there, her heart thumping for fear. She was very near turning back, but then she thought of the Prince and of the human soul, and her courage came back. She bound her long flowing hair close to her head, so that the polypi might not seize it; then she crossed both hands over her breast, and darted through the water as only fishes can, right between the hideous polypi, which stretched out their long supple arms and fingers after her.

And now she came to a large slimy open swamp where sat the hateful sea witch among slimy watersnakes and the bones of shipwrecked men.

"I know what you want!" said the sea-witch; "you're a fool for your pains! Still you shall have your own way, but you will get into trouble, my pretty Princess. You want to be rid of your fish's tail, eh, and to have a couple of stumps to walk about on as men have, so that the young Prince may fall in love with you, and you may get him and a soul into the bargain!"

And with that, the witch laughed loudly and horribly.

"I will brew you a magic drink, and you must swim to land, sit on the shore, and drink it before sunrise. Then your tail will split and shrivel up into what men call nice legs; but it will hurt, mind you, for it will be like a sharp sword piercing you. All who see you will say that you are the loveliest girl they ever saw. You will keep your graceful motion, no dancing girl will be able to move so lightly as you; but every step you take for a time will be to you like treading on sharp knives till the blood flows. If you still choose to suffer all this, I have the power to help you."

"I do," said the little mermaid with a trembling voice; she thought of the Prince and of winning a soul.

"But remember," said the witch, "once you have a girl's form you can never become a mermaid again! You will never be able to dive down through the water to your sisters or go back to your father's palace; and if you should fail to win the Prince's love so that, for your sake, he forgets father and mother and cleaves to you with all his soul, and lets the priest make you man and wife, you will not obtain a soul! If he marries another, your heart will break and you will become mere foam upon the billows!"

"Be it so!" said the little mermaid, but she was as pale as death.

"But you must pay me too," said the witch, "and it will be no small thing either that I ask. You have the loveliest voice of all things here at the bottom of the sea, and you fancy you will enchant him with that, I know; not at all, for you must give that voice to me. I choose to have the best thing you have."

"But if you take my voice," asked the little mermaid, "what have I left?"

"Your lovely form," said the witch, "your light step and your speaking eyes, you can reach a man's heart with them, I suppose? Well, have you lost courage, eh? Put out your little tongue and I will cut it off, and you shall have the precious drink!"

"Be it so, then!" said the little mermaid, and the witch put her kettle on the fire to brew the magic drink. At last, when the drink was ready, it looked like the clearest water!

"Here you are!" said the witch, and cut out the tongue of the little mermaid; so that she could neither sing nor talk.

Then the little mermaid swam to her father's palace; the lights in the long dancing hall had been put out; all within were doubtless asleep; but she dared not visit them now that she was dumb and was about to go away from them forever. Her heart felt as if it must burst for sorrow. She stole into the garden, plucked a flower from each of her sister's flower beds, threw a thousand kisses toward her home and swam up again through the dark blue waters.

The sun had not yet risen when she saw the Prince's palace, and mounted the splendid marble staircase. The moon was shining bright and beautiful. The little mermaid drank the sharp burning potion, and it was as though a two-edged sword pierced through her body; she moaned with agony and lay there as one dead.

When the sun rose over the sea she woke and felt a sharp pang; in front of her stood the handsome young Prince. He fixed his eyes upon her so intently that she cast her own eyes down and saw that her fish tail had gone, and that she had the prettiest little white legs; but she was quite naked, so she wrapped herself in her long, thick hair. The Prince asked who she was and how she had come thither; but she could only look at him with her dark blue eyes mildly and sadly, for she could not speak. Then he took her by the hand and led her into the palace. Every step she took was, as the witch said it would be, as if she were treading on points of needles or sharp

knives, but she willingly bore the pain, and holding
the Prince's hand mounted the staircase as light as a
bubble, so that he and everyone else were amazed at
her light and graceful movements.

She was now dressed in the most costly clothing,
all silk and muslin. None in the whole palace was
so lovely; but she could neither sing nor speak.
Lovely slave girls, clad in silk and gold, came and
sang to the Prince and his royal parents; one of them
sang more sweetly than the rest, and the Prince
clapped his hands and smiled at her. This troubled the
little mermaid. She knew that she herself had sung
far more sweetly, and she thought: "Oh, that he
might know that for the sake of being near him I
have given away my voice forever!"

Then the slave girls danced some light and graceful measures to the loveliest music. At this the little
mermaid lifted her white arms, raised herself on the
tips of her toes, and floated lightly across the floor
as none had ever done before.

Everybody was enchanted with her, especially the
Prince, who called her his little foundling, and she
danced more and more, though every time her feet
touched the floor it was as if she trod on a sharp
knife. The Prince said that she should always be with
him, and she was given leave to sit outside his door
on a velvet cushion.

At night, in the Prince's palace, while others slept,

she would go out on the broad marble steps, for it cooled her burning feet to stand in the cold seawater; and then she thought of the friends she had left in the depths below.

One night her sisters rose arm in arm, singing sorrowfully as they swam in the water. She nodded to them, and they knew her, and told her how unhappy she had made them all by going away.

But every day she became dearer to the Prince; he loved her as one might love a dear, good child; but to make her his queen never entered his mind. Yet his wife she must become, or she could never obtain a soul.

"Do you love me most of all?" the eyes of the little mermaid seemed to ask when he took her in his arms and kissed her fair brow.

"Yes, you are dearest of all to me," said the Prince, "for you have the best heart. You are just like a lovely girl I once saw but shall never see again. I was on a ship which was wrecked, the billows cast me ashore near a holy temple, where many young girls were worshipping. The youngest, who found me on the seashore and saved my life, I only saw twice; she is the only one I could love in this world, but you are like her, you almost drive her image from my mind, she belongs to the temple, but my good fortune has sent you to me instead, and we will never part."

"Alas! he knows not that it was I who saved his life," thought the little mermaid. "I carried him right over the sea to the wood where the holy temple stands, I sat beneath the foam and looked to see if any one would come; I saw the pretty girl whom he loves better than he does me!" And the mermaid drew a deep sigh.

But now came talk that the Prince was to marry the lovely daughter of the neighboring king, and that was why he now set about fitting out a splendid ship.

"I must travel," he said to the little mermaid, "I must see this beautiful Princess; my parents ask it of me; but they shall not force me to bring her home as my bride. I cannot love her; she is not like the lovely girl in the temple whom you are like."

In the moonlight nights, when all on board were asleep save the pilot at the helm, she sat at the side of the ship and looked down through the clear water and seemed to see her father's palace. High above it stood the old grandmother with her silver crown on her head, staring up at the ship's keel through the restless water. Then her sisters came up to the surface and looked sadly at her, wringing their white hands.

The next morning the ship sailed into the port of the neighboring king's splendid capital. The church bells were ringing, trumpets sounded from the tops of the high towers, and soldiers stood in line with waving banners and flashing spears.

But the Princess was not yet there, for she had
been brought up in a temple far away, they said,
where she had learned to be good and wise.

Full of eagerness, the little mermaid waited to see
her; and she was sure, when the Princess finally came,
that a more beautiful face she had never seen.

The Prince was enchanted. "It is you!" he cried,
embracing the Princess, "you who saved me when I
lay almost dead on the seashore!" "I am very
happy!" he said to the little mermaid. "The very
best I dared to hope has come to pass. You too will
be glad at my good fortune, for you love me." And
the little mermaid kissed his hand, but she felt already
that her heart would break.

That evening, after the wedding, the bride and
bridegroom went aboard the ship. Cannons roared
and flags waved, and on the deck was placed a royal
bridal tent of cloth of gold and purple and precious
furs.

The sails swelled out in the breeze, and the ship
glided lightly over the ocean. When it grew dark,
colored lamps were lit, and the sailors danced merrily
on the deck. The little mermaid could not help thinking of the first time she had risen above the sea, and
seen the same gaiety and splendor. She whirled round
and round in the dance, skimming along as the swallow skims when it is pursued, and everyone cheered
her, for never before had she danced so beautifully.
She knew this was the last evening she would ever be

able to see him for whom she had left family and home, given up her lovely voice, and suffered endless pain day by day, without his having even dreamed of it. It was the last night on which she was to breathe the same air as he, to look upon the deep sea and the starlit sky.

When it grew dark and all was still on board, the little mermaid leaned her white arms on the railing and looked toward the east for the rosy dawn; at the first sunbeam, she knew well, she must die.

And now the sun rose out of the sea; its rays fell with gentle warmth upon the cold sea foam, and the little mermaid did not feel the pangs of death. She saw above her hundreds of beautiful shapes were hovering and heavenly music was sounding all about. The little mermaid saw that she now had a body like those about her and it rose higher and higher from out of the foam.

"To whom have I come?" cried she, and her voice sounded like the voices of the other beings, so lovely that no earthly music could equal it.

"To the daughters of the air," they answered. "We have found our way to endless life through good deeds. We heal and refresh the children of men. When for three hundred years we have done all the good in our power, we have souls. You, poor little mermaid, have tried to be good with your whole heart; like us, you have suffered and endured, and raised yourself into a spirit of the air. You, too, can win for yourself a soul after three hundred years of good deeds."

And the little mermaid raised her bright arms toward the sun, and for the first time felt tears in her eyes.

There were life and bustle on board the ship again; she saw the Prince and his beautiful bride looking for her, and then sadly down upon the foam, as if they knew she had plunged into the billows. Unseen by either of them, she kissed the bride's forehead, smiled upon the Prince, and rose with the other children of the air up to the rosy clouds which were sailing the sky.

"For three hundred years we shall float and float till we glide into God's kingdom."

"Yes, and we may get there still sooner," whispered one. "Unseen we enter the houses of men where there are children, and when we find a good child who gladdens his parents' hearts, and deserves their love, God shortens our time of trial. The child does not know when we fly through the room, but when we can smile with joy over it, a whole year is taken from the three hundred. But whenever we see a selfish or dishonest child we shed tears of sorrow, and every tear adds a day to our time of trial!"

The Candles ⌒

THERE was a large wax light which was very proud of itself.

"I was born in wax and made in a mould," it said; "I shine better and burn longer than other lights; my place is in the chandelier or the silver candlestick!"

"That must be delightful!" said the tallow candle. "I am only of tallow, only a dip, but I always console myself by remembering that at any rate, I am something more than a rush light; *that* is only dipped twice, while I am dipped four times to give me my thickness. I am quite satisfied; no doubt it is luckier to be born in wax and not in tallow, but one does not order one's place in the world. *They* get into the glass chandelier in the dining room. I stay in the kitchen, but the kitchen is a good place too; the whole house gets its food from there."

"But there is something more important than food," said the wax candle. "Society! To see people shine and to shine oneself! There will be a

52

ball here this evening. Now you'll see that I and all my family will be sent for at once!"

Scarcely had this been said when all the wax candles were sent for, but the tallow candle came along with them too. The lady of the house herself held it in her dainty hand and carried it into the kitchen; there stood a little boy with a basket which was filled with potatoes and apples. All this the good lady gave to the poor boy.

"And there's a candle for you, my little friend!" said she; "your mother works right through the night; she can make use of it!"

The little daughter of the house stood close by and when she heard the words "right through the night," she said with hearty joy: "I shall be up all night, too; we are going to have a ball, and I shall have my large red bows on." How her face beamed! No wax candle can shine like those child-eyes!

So the tallow candle was laid beneath the basket-lid and the boy went away with it.

"I wonder where I am going now" thought the candle. "I am on my way to poor people; perhaps I shall get a brass holder, while the wax-candle sits in silver and sees the most elegant people. How delightful it must be to shine before the grand folk. But it is my lot to be tallow, not wax!"

And the candle came to the poor people, a widow with three children in a little low room right opposite the rich house. "God bless the good lady for what she gave!" said the mother; " 'tis really a lovely light. It may last the whole night." And the candle was lit.

"Fut-foi" it spluttered. "That *was* a nasty-smelling sulphur match she lit me with. That's not the sort of thing they would be likely to offer the wax candle in the rich house over the way"

There, too, candles were lit. They shone over the street; the carriages rumbled along with the smartly dressed ball guests and the music sounded.

"Now they are beginning over there," said the tallow candle, and it thought of the little rich girl's beaming face, more beaming than all the wax lights. "I shall never see *that* sight again!"

Then the smallest of the children of that poor house came in; a little girl. She put her arms round the necks of her brother and sister; she had something very important to tell them, so important that it must be whispered: "This—evening—we—are—going—to—have—only fancy!—we—are—going to—have—*hot potatoes!*"

And her face beamed with delight; the candle shone on it; it saw there a joy, a happiness, as great as in the rich house yonder where the little girl had said, "We are to have a ball this evening, and I shall have my large red bows on!"

"Is it such a great thing to have hot potatoes!"

thought the candle; "there's just as much joy among the little ones here as over there!" And it sneezed on the strength of it, that is to say it spluttered, which is as much as a tallow candle *can* do. The table was laid, the potatoes were eaten. Oh, how nice they tasted! It was quite a dinner, and every one got an apple in the bargain, and the smallest child of all said this little verse:

> "Thou God so good, my thanks to Thee
> That thou hast given to me! Amen."

"Wasn't that nicely said, mother?" said the little one right afterward.

"Do not be proud!" said the mother, "you should think about the good God who has fed you!"

The little ones were put to bed, were kissed, and went straight off to sleep; and the mother sat and sewed till late into the night. And the candles shone from the rich house over the way, and the music sounded. The stars twinkled over all the houses, as brightly on the poor as on the rich; there was no difference.

"That was a lovely evening after all!" said the tallow candle. And it thought of the pair of happy children, the one that was lit by the wax candle and the one that was lit by the tallow candle!

The table was laid, the potatoes were eaten. Oh, how nice they tasted!

The Flying Trunk ❧

THERE was once a merchant who was so rich
that he could have paved the whole street, and
a little alley besides, with silver pieces, but he didn't,
for he had other things to do with his money. He
made a dollar with every penny he invested (that's
the sort of merchant *he* was), and then he died.

His son now got all this money and he lived right
merrily, went to fancy balls every night, made kites
out of bonds and banknotes, and played at ducks and
drakes over the water with gold pieces instead of
stones, so that his money was free to go, and go it did,
till at last he had nothing in the world but four pennies, a pair of slippers, and an old dressing-gown.
Now that he was not fit to be seen in the street with
his friends they washed their hands of him altogether;
but one of them, who was better-natured, sent him
an old trunk, with the message, "Pack up" which
was certainly very good advice, but as he had nothing
at all to pack up he sat in the trunk instead.

It was a very wonderful trunk. You had only to press the lock and the trunk set off flying. It did so now. Whisk, up the chimney it flew with him, high above the clouds, farther and farther and farther still; it creaked frightfully and the young man was frightened lest it should go to pieces altogether, in which case he would have turned quite a pretty somersault. But at last he got to the land of the Turks! He hid the trunk in a wood beneath some dried leaves and then went into the town; there was nothing to prevent him from doing that, for among the Turks everybody went about like himself, in dressing-gowns and slippers.

He happened to meet a nurse with a little child. "Listen, Turkish nurse!" said he, "what is that large castle close to the town with the windows all so high?"

"That is where the King's daughter lives!" said she; "it has been promised that she will have great trouble about a lover, and so no young man is allowed to come near her unless the King and Queen come too."

"Thank you!" said the merchant's son; and he went back to the wood, got into the trunk, flew onto the roof of the castle, and crept through the Princess's window.

She lay upon a sofa asleep, and was so pretty that the merchant's son could not help kissing her. She

He got into his trunk again, and flew onto the roof of the palace.

awoke and was quite frightened, but he said he was
the god of the Turks who had come through the air
to her, and that seemed to please her. So they sat
side by side and he told her tales about her eyes; he
said they were like beautiful dark lakes and that
thoughts swam in them like so many little mermaids;
and he made up stories about her forehead, which he
said was like a snow mountain with the loveliest rooms
and pictures; and he told her about the stork that
brings the sweet little children. Yes, indeed, very
pretty stories they were, so he asked the Princess to
marry him, and she said "Yes," at once.

"But," she added, "you must come on Saturday
when the King and Queen are here to tea; they will
be very proud for me to have a Turkish god for my
husband. But see that you have a really lovely story
ready, for that is what my parents are particularly
fond of; my mother likes *her* stories sweet and wise,
while my father likes them jolly—things that make
one laugh!"

"Very well, the only bridal present I shall bring
will be a nice story!" said he, and so he said good-by.
But the Princess gave him a sword set with gold
pieces: it was just what he wanted and he could use
it very nicely.

So he flew away, bought himself a new dressing
gown, and then sat down in the wood and began
making up a story; it was to be ready by Saturday,

and it is not so easy to do that sort of thing to order.

But he was ready with it at last, and by that time it was Saturday. The King and Queen and the whole court were having tea with the Princess, and they were all awaiting him. He was welcomed heartily.

"And now will you tell us a story?" said the Queen, "one that is sweet and wise!"

"But which will make one laugh as well!" said the King.

"Oh, certainly!" said he; and so he told them what you must now listen to very attentively.

"There was once a bundle of matches which were very proud of their family; their 'tree'—that is to say, the great fir tree of which each one of them was a little splinter—had been a huge old tree in the forest. The matches now lay upon the shelf between a tinder box and an old iron pot, and to these they told the story of their youth.

" 'Yes, when we were on the green branch,' said they, 'then we were indeed happy! Every morning and evening we had diamond tea, that is to say, dew. There was sunshine all day in summer, and all the little birds told us stories. We could see very well that we were rich, for the trees with leaves were only dressed up in summer, but our family had the right to wear our needles both summer and winter. Then came the woodcutters; and our family was cut to the ground. But for us this change was not the end of all things; it was a great promotion. The head of the family got a place as mainmast on board a splendid ship, which could sail round the world if it liked; the other branches went elsewhere, and our own little task now is to light candles for the common people—that is why we noble people have come down to the kitchen.'

" 'Well, things are very different with me!' said the iron pot, by the side of which lay the matches, 'ever since I came out in the world I have been scoured and boiled many and many a time! I believe in being solid, and really, I am the first person in the house! My only joy is to lie neat and clean after dinner on the shelf and to have a sensible chat with my comrades; but, excepting the pail, which occasionally goes down into the garden, we always live indoors. Our only newsgatherer is the market basket. Last year there was an old pot with us who was so frightened by its talk that it fell down and dashed itself to pieces. That market basket is a gossip, I can tell you!'

" 'You chatter too much, you do!' said the tinder-box, and the steel struck the flint till it sparkled. 'Shall we have a cheerful afternoon now?'

" 'Yes, let us talk about who is the most nobly born,' said the matches.

" 'No, I don't like talking about myself,' said the pot. 'Let us have an entertainment. I'll begin. I'll tell about something which everyone can understand; one can imagine oneself having the same good time, and that is such fun. "By the Baltic Sea, where the Danish beeches grow—"

" 'That is a nice beginning,' said the plates, 'we know we shall like that story.'

" 'Yes, there I passed the days of my youth in a quiet family; the furniture was waxed, the floor washed, and we had clean curtains every fortnight.'

" 'How interesting you make your story!' said the hearth broom. 'One can be sure at once that it is a lady who tells the story; it sounds so refined.'

" 'Yes, one does feel that!' said the pail, and it took a little skip for pure joy, so that the floor creaked.

"So the pot kept on with its story, and the end was as good as the beginning.

"The plates rattled for joy, and the hearth brush took some green parsley and crowned the pot, for it knew that that would vex the others. 'If I crown her today,' it thought, 'she will crown me tomorrow.'

" 'Now I will dance,' said the fire tongs, and dance it did. How it flung its legs into the air! The old chair cover in the corner split its sides at the sight.

" 'Let me be crowned too!' said the fire tongs, and crowned it was.

" 'A low lot, a low lot after all!' thought the matches.

"And now the teapot was asked to sing, but she said that she had a cold and could only sing when

she was boiling over, but she was making this up; she
would not sing unless she was on the table with the
family.

"Right on the window sill stood an old quill pen
which the servant used to write with; there was
nothing remarkable about it except that it had been
dipped a little too deeply into the inkpot, but of that
it was proud. 'If the teapot won't sing,' it said, 'she
may leave it alone. Outside there is a nightingale
hanging in a cage; it can sing if you like. True it
hasn't learned anything, but we won't speak ill of it
this evening.'

" 'I do not think it is right that such a foreign bird
should be listened to at all,' said the teakettle, who
was the kitchen singer and half sister of the teapot.
'Is it patriotic? That's what I want to know! Let
the market basket decide.'

" 'All I know is that I am very angry!' said the
market basket; 'nobody can imagine how angry I am.
Is this a proper way of passing the evening, I ask?
Would it not be much better to put the house to
rights first? Everyone would then get his own place,
and I should rule the whole roost. Things would be
very different then!'

" 'Yes, let us kick up a row!' they all said. The
same instant the door opened. It was the maid, and
at once they stood still; no one made a sound. But
there was not a pot there which did not know very

well what it could do and how noble it really was.
'Yes, if only I had managed it,' thought each one of
them, 'what a jolly afternoon we should have had!'

"The maid took the matches and struck a light
with them; how they spluttered and burst into flame,
to be sure! 'Now everyone can see,' thought they,
'that we stand first of all! What light, what splendor
is ours!' and so they burned right out."

"That was a beautiful story!" said the Queen. "I
felt just as the matches did in the kitchen. Yes, now
you shall have our daughter."

"Yes, certainly," said the King, "you shall have
our daughter on Monday!" And they spoke to him
in such a friendly way that he felt he was already
one of the family.

So the wedding day was fixed. The evening before
the whole city was lighted; buns and cakes were scattered to all, and the street boys stood on their heads,
whistled through their fingers, and cried "Hurrah!"
It was truly splendid.

"Yes, I must take good care to do something suit-
able!" thought the merchant's son. So he bought
rockets, crackers, and every sort of firework you can
think of, put them in his trunk and then flew up into
the air. How they went off and how they fizzed!
The Turks all skipped into the air at the sight, so that
their slippers flew about their ears; such a shower of
stars they had never seen before. Now they could

well understand that it was the god of the Turks himself who was to marry the Princess.

As soon as the merchant's son came down again
into the wood with his trunk he thought: "I will
just go into the town to learn how everything went
off!" And it was only natural that he should wish
to do so.

Everyone whom he asked about it had seen the af-
fair in his own way, but one and all thought it
charming.

"I saw the god of the Turks himself," said one;
"he had eyes like shining stars and a beard like foam-
ing water."

"He flew in a fiery mantle," said another; "the
loveliest little angels peeped out from the folds of it."

Yes, he heard the most beautiful things about himself, and the day after he was to be married.

And now he went back to the wood to sit on his
trunk—but where was it? The trunk was burnt! A
spark from the fireworks had remained within, the
trunk had caught fire, and was now nothing but ashes.
He could fly no more, he could not go to meet his
bride.

She stood all day on the roof and waited; and most
likely she is still waiting; but he goes round about the
world and tells stories, although they are not as jolly
as the story he told about the matches.

The Ugly Duckling 〜

I T WAS glorious out in the country. It was summer, and the cornfields were yellow, and the
oats were green; the hay had been put up in stacks in
the green meadows, and the stork went about on his
long red legs, and chattered Egyptian, for this was
the language he had learned from his good mother.
All around the fields and meadows were great forests,
and in the midst of these forests lay deep lakes. Yes,
it was really glorious out in the country. In the
midst of the sunshine there lay an old farm, with deep
canals around it, and from the wall down to the water grew great burdocks, so high that little children
could stand upright under the tallest of them. It was
just as wild there as in the deepest wood. Here sat a
Duck upon her nest, for she had to hatch her young
ones; but she was almost tired out before the little
ones came; and then she had so few visitors. The
other ducks liked better to swim about in the canals

than to run up to sit down under a burdock, and cackle with her.

At last one eggshell after another burst open. "Peep! peep!" each cried, and in all the eggs there were little creatures that stuck out their heads.

"Rap! rap!" they said; and they all came rapping out as fast as they could, looking all around them under the green leaves; and the mother let them look as much as they chose, for green is good for the eyes.

"How wide the world is!" said the young ones, for they certainly had much more room now than when they were in the eggs.

"Do you think this is all the world?" asked the mother. "It goes far across the other side of the garden, quite into the parson's field, but I have never been there yet. I hope you are all together," she said, and stood up. "No, I have not all. The largest egg still lies there. How long is that to last? I am really tired of it." And she sat down again.

"Well, how goes it?" asked an old duck who had come to pay her a visit.

"It lasts a long time with that one egg," said the Duck who sat there. "It will not hatch. Now, only look at the others; are they not the prettiest ducks one could possibly see? They are all like their father; the bad fellow never comes to see me."

"Let me see the egg which will not hatch," said

the old visitor. "Believe me, it is a turkey's egg. I was once cheated in that way, and had much anxiety and trouble with the young ones, for they are afraid of the water. I could not get them to go in. I quacked and clucked, but it was no use. Let me see the egg. Yes, that's a turkey's egg! Let it lie there, and teach the other children to swim."

"I think I will sit on it a little longer," said the Duck. "I've sat so long now that I can sit a few days more."

"Just as you please," said the old duck; and she went away.

At last the great egg burst. "Peep! peep!" said the little one, and crept forth. It was very large and very ugly. The Duck looked at it.

"It's a very large duckling," she said; "none of the others look like that; can it really be a turkey chick? Now we shall soon find it out. It must go into the water, even if I have to push it in myself."

The next day the weather was splendidly bright, and the sun shone on all the green trees. The Mother Duck went down to the water with all her little ones. Splash! she jumped into the water. "Quack! quack!" she said, and one duckling after another plunged in. The water closed over their heads, but they came up in an instant, and floated beautifully; their legs went of themselves, and there they were all in the water. The ugly gray one swam with them.

"No, it's not a turkey," she said; "see how well it can use its legs, and how upright it holds itself. It is my own child! On the whole it's quite pretty, if one looks at it rightly. Quack! quack! come with me, and I'll lead you out into the great world, and show you the poultry yard; but keep close to me, so that no one may tread on you, and beware of the cat!"

And so they came into the poultry yard. There was a terrible noise going on in there, for two families were quarreling about an eel's head, and the cat got it after all.

"See, that's how it goes in the world!" said the Mother Duck; and she sharpened her beak, for she too wanted the eel's head. "Only use your legs," she said. "See that you can bustle about, and bow your heads before the old duck yonder. She's the grandest of all here; she's of Spanish blood—that's why she's so fat; and do you see, she has a red rag round her leg; that's something fine, and the greatest honor a duck can enjoy. It shows that one does not want to lose her, and that she's to be looked up to by man and beast. Shake yourselves—don't turn in your toes, a well-brought-up duckling turns its toes quite out, just like father and mother, so! Now bend your necks and say 'Rap!' "

They did so, but the other ducks round about looked at them, and said quite boldly:

"Look there! Now we're to have these hanging on as if there were not enough of us already! And—fie!—how that duckling yonder looks; we won't stand that!" And one duck flew up and bit it in the neck.

"Let it alone," said the mother; "it does no harm to anyone."

"Yes, but it's too large and funny," said the duck who had bitten it; "and it must be beaten."

"Those are pretty children that the mother has there," said the old duck with the rag round her leg. "They're all pretty but that one: that was a failure. I wish she could change it."

"That cannot be done, my lady," replied the Mother Duck. "It is not pretty, but it has a really good heart, and swims as well as any other; I may even say it swims better. I think it will grow up pretty, and become smaller in time; it has lain too long in the egg, and so is not properly shaped." And then she pinched it in the neck, and smoothed its feathers. "It is a drake," she said, "so it does not matter so much. I think he will be very strong; he makes his way already."

"The other ducklings are graceful enough," said the old duck. "Make yourself at home, and if you find an eel's head, you may bring it to me."

And now they were at home. But the poor Duckling which had crept last out of the egg, and looked

so ugly, was bitten and pushed and jeered, as much
by the ducks as by the chickens.

"It is too big!" they all said. And the turkey
cock, who had been born with spurs, and so thought
himself an emperor, blew himself up like a ship in
full sail, and ran straight down upon it; then he gobbled, and grew quite red in the face. The poor Duckling did not know where it should stand; it was sad
because it looked ugly, and was laughed at by the
whole yard.

So it went on the first day, and afterward it became worse and worse. The poor Duckling was
hunted about by everyone, even its brothers and sisters were quite angry with it and said, "If the cat
would only catch you, you ugly creature!" And
the mother said, "If you were only far away!" And
the ducks bit it, and the chickens beat it, and the
girl who had to feed the poultry kicked at it with her
foot.

Then it ran and flew over the fence, and the little
birds in the bushes flew up in fear.

"That is because I am so ugly!" thought the Duckling; and it shut its eyes, but flew on farther; thus it
came out into the great field where the wild ducks
lived. Here it lay the whole night long, and was
tired and sad.

Toward morning the wild ducks flew up, and
looked at their new companion.

"What sort of a one are you?" they asked; and the Duckling turned in every direction, and bowed as well as it could. "You are very ugly!" said the wild ducks. "But we do not care, so long as you do not marry into our family."

Poor thing! It certainly did not think of marrying, and only hoped to be allowed to lie among the reeds and drink some of the swamp water.

Thus it lay two whole days; then there came two wild geese, or really two wild ganders. It was not long since each had crept out of an egg, and that's why they were so saucy.

"Listen, comrade," said one of them. "You're so ugly that I like you. Will you go with us, and become a bird of passage? Near here, in another field, there are a few sweet lovely wild geese, all unmarried, and all of them can say 'Rap!' You've a chance of making your fortune, ugly as you are!"

"Bang! bang!" sounded through the air; and the two ganders fell down dead in the swamp, and the water became blood red. "Bang! bang!" it sounded again, and whole flocks of wild geese rose up from the reeds. And then there was another report. A great hunt was going on. The hunters were lying in wait all round the moor, and some were even sitting up in the branches of the trees, which spread far over the reeds. The blue smoke rose up like clouds among the dark trees, and was wafted far away across the

water; and the hunting dogs came—splash, splash!—
into the swamp, and the rushes and the reeds bent
down on every side. That was a fright for the poor
Duckling! It turned its head, and put it under its
wing; but at that moment a frightful great dog stood
close by the Duckling. His tongue hung far out of
his mouth and his eyes gleamed horrible and ugly; he
thrust out his nose close against the Duckling, showed
his sharp teeth, and—splash, splash!—on he went,
without seizing it.

"Oh, thank Heaven!" sighed the Duckling. "I
am so ugly that even the dog does not want to
bite me!"

And so it lay quite still, while the shots rattled
through the reeds and gun after gun was fired. At
last, late in the day, the noise ceased; but the poor
Duckling did not dare to get up; it waited several
hours before it looked around, and then hurried away
out of the moor as fast as it could. It ran on over
field and meadow, and by that time there was such
a storm raging that it was hard to get from one place
to another.

Toward evening the Duckling came to a little miserable peasant's hut. This hut was so shaky that it
did not know on which side it should fall; and that's
why it remained standing. The storm whistled round
the Duckling in such a way that the poor creature
had to sit down to keep from blowing away, and the

wind grew worse and worse. Then the Duckling saw that one of the hinges of the door had given way, and the door hung so slanting that the Duckling could slip through the crack into the room; and it did so.

Here lived a woman, with her tomcat and her hen. And the tomcat, whom she called Sonnie, could arch his back and purr, he could even give out sparks; but for that one had to stroke his fur the wrong way. The hen had quite little short legs, and so she was called Chickabiddy-short-shanks; she laid good eggs, and the woman loved her as her own child.

In the morning they all saw the strange Duckling, and the tomcat began to purr, and the hen to cluck.

"What's this?" said the woman, and looked all round; but she could not see well, and so she thought the Duckling was a fat duck that had strayed away. "This is a rare prize!" she said. "Now I shall have duck's eggs. I hope it is not a drake. We must find out."

And so the Duckling was let in on trial for three weeks; but no eggs came. And the tomcat was master of the house, and the hen was the lady, and always said, "We and the world!" for she thought they were half the world, and by far the better half. The Duckling thought one might think differently, but the hen said, "Not at all."

"Can you lay eggs?" she asked.

"No."

"Then you'll have the goodness to hold your tongue."

And the tomcat said, "Can you curve your back, and purr, and give out sparks when you are stroked?"

"No."

"Then you must not speak when sensible people are speaking."

The Duckling sat in a corner and was sad; then the fresh air and the sunshine streamed in, and it was so eager to swim on the water, that it could not help telling the hen of it.

"What are you thinking of?" cried the hen. "You have nothing to do, that's why you have these fancies. Purr or lay eggs, and they will pass away."

"But it is so charming to swim on the water!" said the Duckling, "so refreshing to let it close above one's head, and to dive down to the bottom."

"Yes, that must be great fun, truly," said the hen. "I fancy you must have gone crazy. Ask the cat about it—he's the cleverest animal I know—ask him if he likes to swim on the water, or to dive down; I won't speak about myself. Ask our mistress, the old woman; no one in the world is cleverer than she. Do you think she wishes to swim, and to let the water close above her head?"

"You don't understand me," said the Duckling.

"We don't understand you? Then who is to understand you? You surely don't pretend to be cleverer than the tomcat and the woman—I won't say anything of myself. Don't be conceited, child, and be grateful for all the kindness you have had. Did you not get into a warm room, and have you not fallen into company from which you may learn something? But you are a chatterer, and it is not pleasant to be with you. You may believe me, I speak for your good. I tell you disagreeable things, and by that one may always know one's true friends! Only take care that you learn to lay eggs, or to purr and give out sparks!"

"I think I will go out into the wide world," said the Duckling.

"Yes, do," replied the hen.

And the Duckling went away. It swam on the water, and dived, but every creature slighted it because of its ugliness.

Now came the fall. The leaves in the forest turned yellow and brown; the wind caught them so that they danced about, and up in the air it was very cold. The clouds hung low, heavy with hail and snowflakes, and on the fence stood the raven, crying, "Caw! caw!" for cold; yes, it was enough to make one feel cold to think of this.

The poor little Duckling certainly had a very sad time. One evening—the sun was just setting in his beauty—there came a whole flock of great handsome birds out of the bushes; they were dazzlingly white, with long curving necks; they were swans. They uttered a very strange cry, spread forth their glorious great wings, and flew away from that cold region to warmer lands, to fair open lakes. They mounted so high, so high! and the ugly little Duckling had a strange feeling as it watched them. It turned round and round in the water like a wheel, stretched out its neck toward them, and made such a strange loud cry as frightened itself. Oh! it could not forget those beautiful, happy birds; and as soon as it could see them no longer, it dived down to the very bottom, and when it came up again, it was quite beside itself. It did not know the name of those birds, and it did not know where they were flying; but it loved them more than it had ever loved anyone. It was not at all envious of them. How could it think of wishing to be as lovely as they? It would have been glad if only the ducks would endure its company—the poor ugly creature!

And the winter grew cold, very cold! The Duckling had to swim about in the water, to keep it from freezing entirely; but every night the hole in which it swam about became smaller and smaller. It froze so hard that the icy covering crackled, and the Duckling had to use its legs continually to prevent the hole from freezing up. At last it became tired, and lay quite still, and thus froze fast in the ice.

Early in the morning a peasant came by, and when he saw what had happened, he took his wooden shoe,

broke the ice crust to pieces, and carried the Duckling home to his wife. Then it came to itself again.
The children wanted to play with it, but the Duckling thought they wished to hurt it, and in its terror
fluttered up into the milk pan, so that the milk
splashed down into the room. The woman clapped
her hands, at which the Duckling flew down into the
butter tub, and then into the meal barrel and out
again. How it looked then! The woman screamed,
and struck at it with the fire tongs; the children tumbled over one another in their effort to catch the
Duckling, and they laughed and screamed finely!
Happily the door stood open, and the poor creature
was able to slip out between the shrubs into the newly
fallen snow; and there it lay quite tired out.

But it would be too sad if I were to tell all the
misery and trouble which the Duckling had to endure
in the hard winter. It lay out on the field among the
reeds, when the sun began to shine again and the larks
to sing; it was a beautiful spring.

Then all at once the Duckling could flap its wings;
they beat the air more strongly than before, and carried it strongly away; and before it knew how all this
happened, it found itself in a great garden, where the
elder trees smelt sweet, and bent their long green
branches down to the canal that wound past. Oh,
here it was so beautiful, such a gladness of spring!
From the thicket came three glorious white swans;

they rustled their wings, and swam lightly on the water. The Duckling knew the splendid creatures, and felt sad.

"I will fly to them, the royal birds, and they will kill me, because I, that am so ugly, dare to come near them! But what of it! Better to be killed by *them* than to be chased by ducks, and beaten by fowls, and pushed about by the girl who takes care of the poultry yard, and to suffer hunger in winter!" So it flew out into the water and swam toward the beautiful swans; they looked at it, and came sailing down upon it with outspread wings. "Kill me!" said the poor creature, and bent its head down upon the water, expecting nothing but death. But what was this that it saw in the clear water? It saw its own image; and lo! it was no longer a clumsy dark gray bird, ugly and hateful to look at, but—a swan!

It matters nothing if one is born in a duck yard, if one has only lain in a swan's egg.

It felt quite glad at all the need and sorrow it had suffered, now it felt happy in all the splendor about it. And the great swans swam round it, and stroked it with their beaks.

Into the garden came little children, who threw bread and corn into the water; and the youngest cried: "There is a new one!" and the other children shouted joyously, "Yes, a new one has come!" And they clapped their hands and danced about, and ran to their father and mother, and bread and cake were thrown into the water; and they all said, "The new one is the most beautiful of all! so young and handsome!" and the old swans bowed their heads before him.

Then he felt quite ashamed, and hid his head under his wings, for he did not know what to do; he was so happy, and yet not at all proud. He thought how he had been chased and hurt; and now he heard them saying that he was the most beautiful of all birds. Even the elder tree bent its branches down into the water before him, and the sun shone warm and mild. Then his wings rustled, he lifted his slender neck, and cried happily from the depths of his heart:

"I never dreamed of so much happiness when I was the Ugly Duckling!"

The Emperor's New Clothes

MANY years ago there lived an Emperor who was so fond of new clothes that he spent all his money upon dress and finery. He cared not a straw for his soldiers, nor for going to the theater or driving in the park; all he really cared about was showing his new clothes. He had a coat for every hour of the day.

The great city where he lived was a very pleasant place. Many strangers visited it every day, and one day two rogues arrived who said they were weavers, and pretended they knew how to weave the most beautiful cloth. Not only were the colors and patterns unusually fine, they said, but the cloth was so delicate that nobody who was either unfit for his office or stupid could see them.

"They would indeed be valuable clothes," thought the Emperor. "By wearing them, I could find out which of my ministers are unfit for their positions, and I could tell the wise from the stupid. Yes, some of that cloth must be woven for me at once." And he

81

gave the two rogues a lot of money in advance so that they might begin their work.

So they set up two looms and pretended they were working, but there was really nothing at all upon the looms. Very soon they asked for the finest silk and the purest gold thread, which they put carefully away, and worked on with the empty looms till late into the night.

"I should like to know how the clothes are getting on," thought the Emperor; but really and truly he felt a little uneasy when he remembered that the stupid and the unfit would not be able to see the cloth. He fancied, indeed, that he had no need to be anxious on his own account, but he thought it would be safer to send someone else first to see how things went. Every person throughout the city had heard of the wonderful new cloth, and all were eager to see how foolish or stupid their neighbors were.

"I will send my worthy old minister to the weavers," thought the Emperor; "he can best see what the cloth looks like, for he is a man of brains and none is fitter for his office than he."

So the able old minister went into the room where the two rogues sat working at the empty looms. "Mercy on us!" thought he, and opened his eyes very wide. "I can't see anything." But he took very good care not to say so.

The two rogues begged him to draw nearer, and

asked him if the pattern was not a pretty one, and the colors very beautiful. Then they pointed at the empty looms, and the poor old minister opened his eyes wider and wider, but he could see nothing, for there was nothing to see. "Good gracious!" thought he, "I am not stupid, surely? I never thought so before, and I'll take good care that nobody shall know it now. What! I am not fit for my office, eh? Oh, no, it will never do to go and say that I can't see the cloth!"

"Well, have you nothing to say about it?" asked one of the weavers.

"Oh, it is beautiful! the most lovely thing in the world!" said the old minister, and he took out his spectacles. "What a pattern! And those colors, too! Yes, I'll tell the Emperor that it pleases me immensely!"

"Well, we are pleased with it too," said the two weavers; and now they named the colors and described the pattern. The old minister listened carefully to all they said, so as to be able to repeat the same things to the Emperor, which he did.

And now the rogues asked for more money, more silk, and more gold; they needed the gold for the weaving, they said. They stuck everything into their own pockets; not so much as a thread passed over the looms; but they kept on as before weaving upon the empty looms.

In a short time the Emperor sent another very bright officer to see how the weaving was getting on, and if the cloth was nearly ready. He looked and looked, but there was nothing there but the empty loom.

"A pretty piece of cloth, isn't it?" said the two rogues, and pretended to point out the pretty patterns, of which there was really nothing.

"Surely I am not stupid!" thought the man. "Not fit for my position, eh! A pretty joke, I must say, but I must not let it be noticed!" So he praised the cloth he did not see, and praised them for the beautiful colors and the lovely patterns. "Yes, it is perfectly enchanting!" said he to the Emperor.

Soon all the people in the town were talking of the splendid cloth.

And now the Emperor had a mind to see the cloth himself while it was still on the loom. With a host of the great folk of his realm, among whom were the two able officers who had been there before, he went to the two crafty rogues who were now working with all their might, but without a stitch or thread.

"Now, is it not magnificent?" said the two officers. "Will your Majesty notice what patterns, what colors are here?" and they pointed at the empty looms, taking if for granted that the others could see the cloth.

"Why, what is this?" thought the Emperor. "I don't see anything! How horrible! Am I stupid then? Am I unfit to be Emperor? That would be the most frightful thing that could happen to me! Oh, it is very fine!" said he aloud. "It has my most gracious approval!" and he nodded his head, and gazed at the empty loom. He would not say that he could not see anything. His whole suite stared and stared; they could make no more of it than the rest, but they repeated after the Emperor, "Oh, it is very fine!" and advised him to wear clothes made of this new and gorgeous cloth for the first time at the grand procession which was about to take place.

"It is magnificent, elegant, excellent!" went from mouth to mouth. Everybody seemed so mightily pleased with the cloth that the Emperor gave each of the rogues a ribbon and a cross to wear, and conferred on them the title of "Weavers to the Imperial Court."

On the eve of the procession the rogues sat up all night, and had more than sixteen candles lit. The people could see that they were busy getting ready the Emperor's new clothes. They pretended to take the cloth from the loom, they clipped the air with large scissors, and sewed with needles without thread, and at last declared, "There, the clothes are now quite ready!"

The Emperor, with his principal lords, then came himself, and the rogues raised their arms as if they were holding up something, and said, "Look, here are the hose, and here is the coat, and here the mantle. They are as light as gossamer," they continued, "you would fancy you had nothing on at all, but that is just the beauty of the cloth."

"Of course!" said all the gentlemen-in-waiting; but they could see nothing, for there was nothing to see.

"And now, if your Imperial Majesty will most graciously have your clothes taken off," said the rogues, "we will put on the new ones for your Majesty. In front of the large mirror, please! Thank you!"

So the Emperor's clothes were taken off, and the rogues pretended to give him the newly made ones piece by piece, and they smoothed down his body, and tied something fast which was supposed to be the train, and the Emperor turned and twisted himself in front of the mirror.

"What a capital suit it is! How nicely it fits!" the people cried with one voice. "What a pattern! What colors! It is a splendid dress!"

"The canopy which is to be borne over your Majesty in the procession is waiting outside," the Master of the Ceremonies announced.

"All right," said the Emperor; "I am quite ready. Do my clothes fit well?" He turned himself once more before the mirror, to make believe that he was now taking a general look at his splendor. The gentlemen-in-waiting, who had to bear his train, fumbled with their hands along the floor as if they were taking the train up, and as they went along they held their hands in the air, for they dared not let it be supposed that they saw nothing.

And thus the Emperor marched in the procession beneath the beautiful canopy, and every one in the streets and in the windows said, "Gracious! how perfect the Emperor's new clothes are! What a beautiful train! How splendidly everything fits!" No one would have it supposed that he saw nothing, for then he would certainly have been unfit for his post, or very stupid. None of the Emperor's clothes had been so successful as these.

"Why, he has nothing on!" cried a little child.

"Listen to the voice of innocence!" said the father; for everyone was whispering to his neighbor what the child had said. "He has nothing on! There is a little child here who says he has nothing on!"

"He really has nothing on!" at length cried the whole crowd.

The Emperor crouched down as he heard, for it seemed to him that they were right, but he thought at the same time, "At any rate I must go through with this procession to the end." So he put on a still haughtier air, and the gentlemen-in-waiting marched behind, carefully holding up the train that wasn't there.

Great Claus and Little Claus

THERE lived two men in one village, and they had the same name—each was called Claus; but one had four horses, and the other only a single horse. To tell one from the other, folk called him who had four horses Great Claus, and the one who had only a single horse Little Claus. Now we shall hear what happened to each of them, for this is a true story.

The whole week through Little Claus had to plow for Great Claus, and to lend him his one horse; then Great Claus helped him out with all his four, but only once a week, and that on a Sunday. Hurrah! how Little Claus smacked his whip over all five horses, for they were as good as his own on that one day. The sun shone gaily, and all the bells in the steeples were ringing as the people passed by dressed in their best, with their hymn books under their arms. They were going to church to hear the minister preach and they saw Little Claus plowing with five horses; but he was

so merry that he cracked his whip again and again, and
cried, "Gee up, all my five horses!"

"You must not talk so," said Great Claus, "for only
the one horse is yours."

But when no one was passing Little Claus forgot
that he was not to say this, and he cried, "Gee up,
all my horses!"

"Now, I must beg of you to stop that," cried Great
Claus, "for if you say it again, I shall hit your horse
on the head, so that he will fall down dead, and then it
will be all over with him."

"I will not say it any more," said Little Claus.

But when people came by soon afterward, and
nodded "Good day" to him, he became very glad, and
thought it looked very well, after all, that he had five
horses to plow his field; and so he smacked his whip
again, and cried, "Gee up, all my horses!"

"I'll 'gee up' your horses!" said Great Claus. And
he took the hatchet and hit the only horse of Little
Claus on the head, so that he fell down, and was dead.

"Oh, now I haven't any horse at all!" said Little
Claus, and he began to cry.

Then he skinned the horse, and let the hide dry in
the wind, and put it in a sack and hung it over his
shoulder, and went to the town to sell his horse's skin.

He had a very long way to go, and had to pass
through a great dark wood, and the weather became

dreadfully bad. He was lost, and before he got into the right way again it was evening, and it was too far to get home again or even to the town before nightfall.

Close by the road stood a large farmhouse. The shutters were closed outside the windows, but the light could still be seen shining out over them.

"Perhaps they will let me stop here through the night," thought Little Claus; and he went to the door and knocked.

The farmer's wife opened the door; but when she heard what he wanted she told him to go away, saying that her husband was not at home, and she would not take in strangers.

"Then I shall have to sleep outside," said Little Claus. And the farmer's wife shut the door in his face.

Close by stood a great haystack, and between this and the farmhouse was a little shed thatched with straw.

"Up there I can lie," said Little Claus, when he looked up at the roof; "that is a capital bed. I suppose the stork won't fly down and bite me in the legs." For a living stork was standing on the roof, where he had his nest.

Now Little Claus climbed up to the roof of the shed, where he lay, and turned round to settle himself comfortably. The wooden shutters did not cover the windows at the top, and he could look straight into

the room of the house. There was a great table, with
the cloth laid, and wine and roast meat and a glorious
fish upon it. The farmer's wife and the sexton were
seated at the table, and nobody else. She was filling
his glass, and he was digging his fork into the fish, for
that was his favorite dish.

"If I could only get some too!" thought Little
Claus, as he stretched out his head toward the window.
Heavens! what a glorious cake he saw standing there!
Yes, certainly, that *was* a feast.

Now he heard someone riding along the high road.
It was the woman's husband, who was coming home.
He was a good man enough, but he could never bear
to see a sexton. If a sexton appeared before his eyes
he became very angry. And that was the reason why
the sexton had gone to the wife to wish her "Good
day" when he knew that her husband was not at
home; and so the good woman put the best fare she
had before him. But when they heard the man coming they were frightened, and the woman begged the
sexton to creep into a great empty chest which stood
there; and he did so, for he knew the husband could
not bear the sight of a sexton. The woman quickly
hid all the good meat and wine in her baking-oven; for
if her husband had seen that, he would have been certain to ask what it meant.

"Ah, yes!" sighed Little Claus, up on his shed roof
when he saw all the good food being put away.

"Is there anyone up there?" asked the farmer; and
he looked up Little Claus. "Who are you lying there?
Better come with me into the room."

And Little Claus told him how he had lost his way,
and asked if he could stay there for the night.

"Yes, certainly," said the farmer, "but first we must
have something to live on."

The woman spoke to them both in a very friendly
way, spread the cloth on a long table, and gave them
a great dish of porridge. The farmer was hungry,
and ate with a good appetite; but Little Claus could
not help thinking of the capital roast meat, fish, and
cake which he knew were in the oven. Under the
table, at his feet, he had laid the sack with the horse's
hide in it; you remember that he had come out to sell
it in the town. He could not relish the porridge.
Then a bright idea came to him and he trod upon the
sack until the dry skin inside crackled quite loudly.

"Why, what have you in your sack?" asked the
farmer.

"Oh, that's a magician," answered Little Claus.
"He says we are not to eat porridge, for he has given
us the oven full of roast meat, fish, and cake."

"Wonderful!" cried the farmer; and he opened the
oven in a hurry, and found all the dainty food which
his wife had hidden there, but which, as he thought,
the wizard had sent them. The woman dared not say
anything, but put the things at once on the table; and

so they both ate of the meat, the fish, and the cake. Now Little Claus again trod on his sack, and made the hide creak.

"What does he say now?" said the farmer.

"He says," replied Claus, "that he has given us three bottles of wine too, and that they are standing there in the corner behind the oven."

Now the woman had to bring out the wine which she had hidden, and the farmer drank it and became very merry. He would have been very glad to see such a magician as Little Claus had there in the sack.

"Can he send the demon out?" asked the farmer. "I should like to see him, for now I am merry."

"Oh, yes," said Little Claus, "my magician can do anything that I ask of him. Can you not?" he asked, and trod on the hide, so that it crackled. "He says 'Yes.' But the demon is very ugly to look at, we had better not see him."

"Oh, I'm not at all afraid. Pray, what will he look like?"

"Why, he'll look the very image of a sexton."

"Ha!" said the farmer, "that *is* ugly! You must know, I can't bear the sight of a sexton. But it doesn't matter now, for I know that he's a demon, so I shall easily stand it. Now I have courage, but he must not come too near me."

"Now I will ask my magician," said Little Claus; and he trod on the sack and held his ear down.

"What does he say?"

"He says you may go and open the chest that stands in the corner, and you will see the demon crouching in it; but you must hold the lid so that he doesn't slip out."

"Will you help me to hold him?" asked the farmer. And he went to the chest where the wife had hidden the real sexton, who sat in there and was very much afraid. The farmer opened the lid a little way and peeped in underneath it.

"Ha!" he cried, and sprang backward. "Yes, now I've seen him, and he looked exactly like our sexton. Oh, that was dreadful!"

Upon this they must drink. So they sat and drank until late into the night.

"You must sell me that magician," said the farmer. "Ask as much as you like for him; I'll give you a whole bushel of money directly."

"No, that I can't do," said Little Claus, "only think how much use I can make of him."

"Oh, I should so much like to have him!" cried the farmer, and he went on begging.

"Well," said Little Claus at last, "as you have been so kind as to give me shelter for the night, I will let it be so. You shall have him for a bushel of money; but I must have the bushel heaped up."

"That you shall have," replied the farmer. "But you must take the chest yonder away with you. I will not keep it in my house an hour. One cannot know—perhaps he may be there still."

Little Claus gave the farmer his sack with the dry hide in it, and got a whole bushel of money, and that heaped up. The farmer also gave him a big cart, in which to carry off his money and chest.

"Good-by!" said Little Claus, and he went off with his money and the chest, in which the sexton was still sitting.

On the other side of the wood was a great deep river. The water rushed along so rapidly that one could scarcely swim against the stream. A fine new bridge had been built over it. Little Claus stopped on the middle of the bridge, and said quite loud, so that the sexton could hear:

"Oh, what shall I do with this stupid chest? It's as heavy as if stones were in it. I shall only get tired if I drag it any farther, so I'll throw it into the river; if it drifts home to me well and good, and if it does not, it will be no great matter."

And he took the chest with one hand, and lifted it up a little, as if he intended to throw it into the river.

"No! stop!" cried the sexton from within the chest; "let me out first!"

"Hullo!" exclaimed Little Claus, pretending to be frightened, "he's in there still! I must make haste and throw him into the river, that he may be drowned."

"Oh, no, no!" screamed the sexton. "I'll give you a whole bushelful of money if you'll let me go."

"Why, that's another thing!" said Little Claus; and he opened the chest.

The sexton crept quickly out, pushed the empty chest into the water, and went to his house, where Little Claus got a whole bushelful of money. He had already taken one from the farmer, and so now he had his cart loaded with money.

"See, I've been well paid for the horse," he said to himself when he had got home to his own room, and was emptying all the money into a heap in the middle of the floor. "That will vex Great Claus when he hears how rich I have grown through my one horse; but I won't tell him how."

So he sent a boy to Great Claus to ask for a bushel measure.

"What can he want with it?" thought Great Claus. And he smeared some tar inside the measure, so that some part of whatever was measured should stick to it. And thus it happened that when he received the measure back, there were three new eight-shilling pieces stuck fast in it.

"What's this?" cried Great Claus; and he ran off at once to Little Claus. "Where did you get all that money?"

"Oh, that's for my horse's skin. I sold it yesterday evening."

"That's really being well paid," said Great Claus. And he ran home in a hurry, took an ax, and killed all his four horses; then he skinned them, and carried off their skins to the town.

"Hides! hides! who'll buy any hides?" he cried through the streets.

All the shoemakers and tanners came running, and asked how much he wanted for them.

"A bushel of money for each!" said Great Claus.

"Are you mad?" said they. "Do you think we have money by the bushel?"

"Hides! hides!" he cried again, and to all who asked him what the hides would cost he replied, "A bushel of money."

"He wants to make fools of us," they all exclaimed. And the shoemakers took their straps, and the tanners their aprons, and they began to beat Great Claus.

"Hides! hides!" they called after him, jeeringly. "Yes, we'll tan your hide for you. Out of the town with him!" And Great Claus made the best haste he could, for he had never yet been thrashed as he was thrashed now.

"Well," said he when he got home, "Little Claus shall pay for this."

So he took the biggest sack he could find, and went over to Little Claus, and said, "You've tricked me! But you shall never trick me any more." And he seized Little Claus round the body, and thrust him into the sack, and took him upon his back, and called out to him as he started off, "Now I shall go off with you and drown you."

It was a long way that he had to travel before he came to the river, and Little Claus was not light to carry. The road led him close to a church; the organ was playing, and the people were singing so beautifully! Then Great Claus put down his sack, with Little Claus in it, close to the church door, and thought it would be a very good thing to go in and hear a psalm before he went farther; for Little Claus could not get out, and all the people were in church; and so he went in.

"Ah, yes! yes!" sighed Little Claus in the sack. And he turned and twisted, but he found he could not loosen the cord. Then there came by an old drover with snow-white hair, and a great staff in his hand; he was driving a whole herd of cows and oxen before him, and they stumbled against the sack in which Little Claus was shut, so that it was tipped over.

"Oh, dear!" sighed Little Claus, "I'm so young yet, and am to go to heaven now!"

"And I, poor fellow," said the drover, "am so old already, and can't get there yet!"

"Open the sack," cried Little Claus; "creep into it instead of me, and you will get to heaven directly."

"With all my heart," replied the drover; and he untied the sack, out of which Little Claus crept forth.

"But will you look after the cattle?" said the old man; and he crept into the sack at once, so Little Claus tied it up, and went his way with all the cows and oxen.

Soon afterward Great Claus came out of the church. He took the sack on his shoulders again, although it seemed to him as if the sack had become lighter; for the old drover was only half as heavy as Little Claus.

"How light he is to carry now! Yes, that is because I have heard a psalm."

So he went to the river, which was deep and broad, threw the sack with the old drover in it into the water, and called after him, thinking that it was Little Claus. "You lie there! Now you shan't trick me any more!"

Then he went home; but when he came to a place where there was a crossroad, he met Little Claus driving all his cattle.

"What's this?" cried Great Claus. "Have I not drowned you?"

"Yes," replied Little Claus, "you threw me into the river less than half an hour ago."

"But where did you get all those fine beasts from?" asked Great Claus.

"These beasts are sea cattle," replied Little Claus. "I'll tell you the whole story—and thank you for drowning me, for now I'm at the top of the tree. I am really rich! How frightened I was when I lay huddled in the sack, and the wind whistled about my ears when you threw me down from the bridge into the cold water! I sank to the bottom immediately; but I was not hurt, for the most splendid soft grass grows down there. Upon that I fell; and immediately the sack was opened, and the loveliest girl, with a snow-white dress and a green wreath upon her wet hair, took me by the hand, and said, 'Are you come, Little Claus? Here you have some cattle to begin with. A mile farther along the road there is a whole herd more, which I will give to you.' And now I saw that the river formed a great road for the people of the sea. Down in its bed they walked and drove right from the sea, and straight into the land, to where the river ends. There it was so beautifully full of flowers and of the freshest grass; the fishes, which swam in the water, shot past my ears, just as here the birds in the air. What pretty people there were there, and what fine cattle pasturing on mounds and in ditches!"

"But why did you come up again to us so soon?" asked Great Claus. "I should not have done that, if it is so beautiful down there."

"Why," replied Little Claus, "that shows how wise I am. You heard me tell you that the sea girl said, 'A mile farther along the road'—and by the road she meant the river, for she can't go anywhere else—'there is a whole herd of cattle for you.' But I know what bends the stream makes—sometimes this way, sometimes that; there's a long way to go round: no, the thing can be managed in a shorter way by coming here to the land, and driving across the fields toward the river again. In this way I save myself almost half a mile, and get all the quicker to my seacattle!"

"Oh, you are a fortunate man!" said Great Claus. "Do you think I should get some sea cattle too if I went down to the bottom of the river?"

"Yes, I think so," replied Little Claus. "But I cannot carry you in the sack as far as the river; you are too heavy for me! But if you wish to go there, and creep into the sack yourself, I will throw you in with a great deal of pleasure."

"Thanks!" said Great Claus; "but if I don't get any sea cattle when I am down there, I shall beat you, you may be sure!"

"Oh, no; don't be so fierce!"

And so they went together to the river. When the beasts, which were thirsty, saw the stream, they ran as fast as they could to get at the water.

"See how they hurry!" cried Little Claus. "They are eager to get back to the bottom."

"Yes, but help me first!" said Great Claus, or else you shall be beaten."

And so he crept into the great sack which Little Claus held for him.

"Put a big stone in, for I'm afraid I shan't sink else," said Great Claus.

"That can be done," replied Little Claus; and he

F.R

"Put a big stone in, for I'm afraid I shan't sink else,"
said Great Claus.

put a big stone into the sack, tied the rope tightly, and pushed against it. *Plump!* There lay Great Claus in the river, and sank at once to the bottom.

"I'm afraid he won't find the cattle!" said Little Claus; and then he drove homeward with what he had.

The Nightingale ✑

MANY years ago there was an Emperor in China who lived in a splendid palace. He was very proud of his palace and was greatly pleased when travelers came from all over the world to see it. These travelers wrote many books about it, but they also wrote about a Nightingale which sang beautifully in the forest nearby.

The Emperor had never heard of the Nightingale till he read about it in a book. Then he called his servants. "Why has no one ever told me about this wonderful singing bird?" he said. "Bring it to me and let the bird sing for me this evening."

But his men had never seen the bird, and no one in the court knew anything about it. At last, in the kitchen, they came upon a poor little girl, one of the lowest of the cooks, who said, "Oh, dear me, yes. I know the Nightingale well. Oh, how she sings! The poor fishermen know her well. And every night when I am going through the forest to my mother's home it sings for me very sweetly."

Gladly the girl offered to take the king's servants to the forest, and hardly had they entered the woods, when the Nightingale began to sing. The men listened in wonder. Never before had they heard such music.

"Little Nightingale," the girl cried out, quite loud, "our most gracious Emperor wishes so much that you sing for him."

"With the greatest pleasure," answered the Nightingale.

So saying the bird flew in front of them, and they all went back to the palace. The whole court was present, and even the little kitchen maid was permitted to stand by the Emperor's chair.

Then the Nightingale hopped merrily upon a golden perch and began to sing. It sang so sweetly that great tears came into the Emperor's eyes. "Stay with us, little Nightingale," he cried, "and you shall have everything you wish."

"I will stay," said the Nightingale, "but I am paid enough. I have seen tears in the Emperor's eyes."

So it came to pass that the Nightingale had a splendid cage and was given everything that she wished.

One day came a package marked "The Nightingale," and when they opened it they found a clockwork bird, covered with diamonds and precious stones. When it was wound up it sang, just like the real bird. Round its neck was a ribbon on which was written, "From the Emperor of Japan to the Emperor of China."

"Oh, this is splendid!" cried the ladies and gentlemen of the court. Even the Emperor was delighted, and again and again the clockwork Nightingale sang. The real Nightingale stole away to the forest again, and you may imagine how glad the woodcutters and fishermen were when they heard the sweet song once more.

Five years passed away, when the whole land was thrown into deep grief by the Emperor's sickness, and the doctors said he was close to death. As they leaned over the dying Emperor they heard him whisper, "Music! Music! Make the clockwork bird sing."

But alas, something had gone wrong with the works of the clockwork bird, and no one could fix it; no one could make it sing. Then when it seemed as if nothing could be done, there sounded the most delightful song. It was the little live Nightingale. She had heard of the Emperor's distress and had come to cheer him. As she sang, he felt his strength coming back, and clasping his hands together he said, "Oh, Nightingale, come back to us. I will break the clockwork bird in pieces."

"No, you must not do that," said the Nightingale. "The poor little make-believe bird did as well as it could, so don't punish it."

"And will you come back to your cage?" asked the Emperor.

"No," said the Nightingale. "I must share my song with the poor woodcutters and the fishermen. But I will come every night and sing you one song, and you will grow strong and well. Now go to sleep, and wake refreshed."

The Emperor fell into a deep sleep so that his attendants thought he had indeed passed away. But in the morning he opened his eyes, and looking around at the sorrowful people, he said "Good morning."

And then what a great rejoicing there was in the land! For the Emperor was well and strong again. And every night the windows of the palace were thrown open wide to hear the lovely song of the Nightingale.

The Traveling Companion

POOR John was very sad, for his father was ill and he had no hope of his getting well. John sat alone with the sick man in the little room, and the lamp had nearly burnt out, for it was late in the night.

"You have been a good son, John," said the sick father, "and God will help you on in the world." He looked at him, as he spoke, with mild, gentle eyes, drew a long breath, and died so quietly it seemed as if he still slept.

John cried bitterly. He had no one in the wide world now; neither father, mother, brother nor sister. Poor John! he knelt down by the bed, kissed his dead father's hand, and wept many, many bitter tears. But at last his eyes closed, and he fell asleep with his head resting against the hard bed-post.

Then he dreamed a strange dream; he thought he saw the sun shining upon him, and his father alive and well, and even heard him laughing as he used to do when he was very happy. A beautiful girl, with a golden crown on her head, and long, shining hair, gave him her hand; and his father said, "See what a lovely bride you have won. She is the loveliest girl on the whole earth." Then he awoke, and all the beautiful things were gone and his father lay dead on the bed, and he was all alone. Poor John!

During the following week the dead man was buried. The son walked behind the coffin which held his father, whom he so dearly loved, and he would never see again. He heard the earth fall on the coffin lid, and watched it till only a corner was in sight, and at last that also was hidden. He felt as if his heart would break with its sorrow, till those who stood round the grave sang a psalm, and the sweet, holy tones brought tears into his eyes, which helped him. The sun shone brightly down on the green trees, as if it would say, "You must not be so sad, John. Do you see the beautiful blue sky above you? Your father is up there, and he prays to the loving Father of all, that you may do well in the future."

"I will always be good," said John, "and then I shall go to be with my father in heaven. What joy it will be when we see each other again! How much I shall have to tell him, and how many things he will be able to tell me of the joys of heaven, and teach me as he once did on earth. Oh, how happy it will be!"

He could see it all so plainly that he smiled even while the tears ran down his cheeks.

The little birds in the chestnut trees twittered, "Tweet, tweet"; they were so happy, although they had seen the funeral; but they seemed as if they knew that the dead man was now in heaven, and that he had wings much larger and more beautiful than their own; that he was happy now, because he had been good here on earth, and they were glad of it. John saw them fly away out of the green trees into the wide world, and he longed to fly with them; but first he cut out a large wooden cross, to place on his father's grave; and when he brought it there in the evening, he found the grave decked out with gravel and flowers. Strangers had done this; they who had known the good old father who was now dead, and who had loved him very much.

Early the next morning John packed up his little bundle of clothes, and placed all his money, fifty dollars and a few pennies, in his girdle; with this he started out in the world. But first he went into the church-yard; and, by his father's grave, he offered up a prayer, and said, "Good-by, dear father!"

As he passed through the fields all the flowers looked fresh and beautiful in the warm sunshine, and nodded in the wind, as if they wished to say, "Welcome to the greenwood, where all is fresh and bright."

Then John turned to have one more look at the old church, in which he had been christened, and where his father had taken him every Sunday to hear the service and join in singing the psalms. As he looked at the old tower, he saw the bell ringer standing at one of the narrow openings, with his little pointed red cap on his head, and shading his eyes from the sun with his bent arm. John nodded good-by to him, and the little ringer waved his red cap round his head, laid his hand on his heart, and kissed his hand to him a great many times, to show that he felt kindly toward him, and wished him a pleasant journey.

John kept on his way, and thought of all the wonderful things he should see in the great beautiful world, till he found himself farther away from home than ever he had been before. He did not even know the names of the places he passed through, and could scarcely understand the people he met, for he was far away in a strange land.

The first night he slept on a haystack, out in the fields, for there was no other bed for him; but it seemed to him so nice and comfortable that even a king need not wish for a better. The field, the brook, the haystack, with blue sky above, formed a beautiful sleeping room. The green grass, with the little red and white flowers, was the carpet; the elder bushes and the hedges of wild roses looked like bouquets on the walls; and for a bath he had the clear, fresh water of the brook; while the rushes bowed their heads to him to wish him good morning and good evening. The moon, like a large lamp, hung high up in the blue ceiling, and he had no fear of its setting fire to his curtains. John slept here quite safely all night; and when he awoke the sun was up, and all the little birds were singing round him, "Good morning, good morning. Are you not up yet?"

It was Sunday, and the bells were ringing for church. As the people went in, John followed them; he heard God's word, joined in singing the psalms, and listened to the preacher. It seemed to him just as if he were in his own church, where he had been christened, and had sung the psalms with his father. Out in the churchyard were several graves, and on some of them the grass had grown very high. John thought of his father's grave, which he knew at last would look like these, if he was not there to weed and attend to it. Then he set to work, pulled up the high grass, raised the wooden crosses which had fallen down, and put back the wreaths which had been blown away from their places by the wind, thinking all the time, "Perhaps someone is doing the same for my father's grave, as I am not there to do it."

Outside the church door stood an old beggar, leaning on his crutch. John gave him his silver money, and then went on his way feeling lighter and happier than ever. Toward evening the weather became very stormy, and he hurried on as quickly as he could to get shelter; but it was quite dark by the time he reached a little lonely church which stood on a hill.

"I will go in here," he said, "and sit down in a corner; for I am quite tired, and want rest."

So he went in, and seated himself; then he folded his hands, and offered up his evening prayer, and was soon fast asleep and dreaming, while the thunder rolled and the lightning flashed outside. When he awoke, it was still night; but the storm was over, and the moon shone in upon him through the windows. Then he saw an open coffin standing in the center of the church, which held a dead man, waiting for burial. John was not at all afraid for he knew also that the dead can never harm anyone. It is living wicked men who do harm to others. Two such bad persons stood now by the dead man, who had been brought to the church to be buried. They meant to throw the poor dead body outside the church door, and not leave him to rest in his coffin.

"Why do you do this?" asked John, when he saw what they were going to do; "it is very wrong. Leave him to rest in peace, in Christ's name."

"Nonsense," replied the two dreadful men. "He has cheated us; he owed us money which he could not pay, and now he is dead we shall not get a penny; so we mean to let him lie like a dog outside the church door."

"I have only fifty dollars," said John, "it is all I have in the world, but I will give it to you if you will promise me faithfully to leave the dead man in peace.

I shall be able to get on without the money; I have strong and healthy limbs, and God will always help me."

"Why, of course," said the horrid men, "if you will pay his debt we will both promise not to touch him. You may depend upon that"; and then they took the money he gave them, laughed at him for his good nature, and went their way.

John laid the dead body back in the coffin, folded the hands, and took leave of it; and went away contentedly through the great forest. All around him he could see the prettiest little elves dancing in the moonlight, which shone through the trees. They were not disturbed by him, for they knew he was good and harmless. It is only bad people who can never see the fairies. Some of them were not taller than the breadth of a finger, and they wore golden combs in their long, yellow hair. They were rocking themselves two together on the large dew drops with which the leaves and the high grass were sprinkled. Sometimes the dew drops would roll away, and then they fell down between the stems of the long grass, and caused a great deal of laughing and noise among the other little people. It was quite charming to watch them at play. Then they sang songs, and John remembered that he had learned those pretty songs when he was a little boy. Large speckled spiders, with silver crowns on their heads, were busy spinning suspension bridges and palaces from one hedge to another, and when the tiny drops fell upon them, they glittered in the moonlight like shining glass. This kept on till sunrise. Then the little elves crept into the flower buds, and the wind seized the bridges and palaces, and fluttered them in the air like cobwebs.

As John left the wood, a strong man's voice called after him, "Hallo, comrade, where are you traveling?"

"Into the wide world," he replied; "I am only a poor boy, I have neither father nor mother, but God will help me."

"I am going into the wide world also," said the stranger; "shall we go together?"

"With all my heart," said he, and so they went on together. Soon they began to like each other very much, for they were both good; but John found out that the stranger was much more clever than himself. He had traveled all over the world, and could tell about almost everything.

The sun was high in the heavens when they seated themselves under a large tree to eat their breakfast, and at the same moment an old woman came toward them. She was very old and almost bent double. She leaned upon a stick and carried on her back a bundle of firewood, which she had picked up in the forest; her apron was tied round it, and John saw three great stems of fern and some willow twigs peeping out. Just as she came close up to them, her foot slipped and she fell to the ground screaming loudly. Poor woman, she had broken her leg! John wanted to carry the old woman home to her cottage; but the stranger opened his knapsack and took out a box, in which he said he had a salve that would quickly make her leg well and strong again, so that she would be able to walk home herself, as if her leg had never been broken. And all that he would ask was the three fern stems which she was carrying in her apron.

"That is rather too high a price," said the old woman, nodding her head quite strangely. She did not seem at all to want to part with the fern stems. But it was not very pleasant to lie there with a broken leg, so she gave them to him; and the ointment was so powerful that no sooner had he rubbed her leg with it than the old woman rose up and walked even better than she had done before. But then this wonderful ointment could not be bought at a chemist's.

"What can you want with those three fern rods?" asked John of his fellow traveler.

"Oh, they will make good brooms," said he; "and I like them because I have strange notions sometimes." Then they walked on together for a long distance.

"How dark the sky is becoming," said John; "and look at those thick, heavy clouds."

"Those are not clouds," replied his fellow traveler, "they are mountains—great, high mountains—on the tops of which we should be above the clouds, in the pure, free air. Believe me, it is delightful up there; tomorrow we shall just reach them."

But the mountains were not so near as they looked; they had to travel a whole day before they reached them, and pass through black forests and piles of rock as large as a town. The journey had been so tiring that John and his fellow traveler stopped to rest at a roadside inn, so that they might gain strength for their journey on the morrow. In the large public room of the inn a great many persons were waiting to see a play performed by dolls. The showman had just put up his little theater, and the people were sitting round the room to see the show. Right in front, in the very best place, sat a stout butcher, with a great bulldog by his side who seemed very much as if he would bite. He sat staring with all his eyes, and so indeed did everyone else in the room.

And then the play began. It was a pretty piece with a king and queen in it, who sat on a beautiful throne, and had gold crowns on their heads. The trains to their dresses were very long, according to the fashion; while the prettiest of wooden dolls with glass eyes and large moustaches, stood at the doors, and opened and shut them, that the fresh air might come into the room. It was a very pleasant play, not at all mournful; but just as the queen stood up and walked across the stage, the big bulldog, who should have been held back by his master, made a spring forward, and caught the queen in his teeth by the slender waist, so that it snapped in two. This was very dreadful.

The poor man, who was showing the dolls, was much distressed, and quite sad about his queen; she was the prettiest doll he had, and the bulldog had broken her head and shoulders off. But after all the people were gone away, the stranger, who came with John, said that he could soon set her to rights. And then he brought out his box and rubbed the doll with some of the salve with which he had cured the old woman when she broke her leg. As soon as this was done the doll's back became quite right again; her head and shoulders were fixed on, and she could even move her limbs herself; there was now no need to pull the wires, for the doll acted just like a living creature, excepting that she could not speak. The man to whom the show belonged was quite delighted at having a doll who could dance of herself without being pulled by the wires; none of the other dolls could do this.

During the night, when all the people at the inn were gone to bed, someone was heard to sigh so deeply and painfully, and the sighing kept up for so long a time, that everyone got up to see what could be the matter. The showman went at once to his little theater and found that it came from the dolls, who all lay on the floor sighing piteously, and staring with their glass eyes; they all wanted to be rubbed with the ointment, so that, like the queen, they might be able to move of themselves. The queen threw herself on her knees, took off her beautiful crown, and, holding it in her hand, cried, "Take this from me, but do rub my husband and his courtiers."

The poor man who owned the theater could hardly keep from crying; he was so sorry that he could not help them. Then he spoke to John's comrade, and promised him all the money he might take in at the next evening's performance, if he would only rub the ointment on four or five of his dolls. But the fellow traveler said he did not want anything excepting the sword which the showman wore by his side. As soon as he got the sword he anointed six of the dolls with the ointment, and they were at once able to dance so gracefully that all the living girls in the room could not help joining in the dance. The coachman danced with the cook, and the waiters with the chamber-maids, and all the strangers joined; even the tongs and the fire shovel tried, but they fell down after the very first jump. So after all it was a very merry night.

The next morning John and his companion left the inn to keep on their journey through the great pine forests and over the high mountains. They got at last so high that towns and villages lay beneath them, and the church steeples looked like little specks be-tween the green trees. They could see for miles around, far away to places they had never visited, and John saw more of the beautiful world than he had ever known before. The sun shone brightly in the blue sky above, and through the clear mountain air came the sound of the huntsman's horn, and the soft sweet notes brought tears into his eyes, and he could not help crying out, "How good and loving God is to give us all this beauty and loveliness in the world to make us happy!"

His fellow traveler stood by with folded hands, looking on the dark woods and the towns bathed in the warm sunshine. Just then there sounded over their heads sweet music. They looked up, and saw a large white swan hovering in the air, and singing as never bird sang before. But the song soon became weaker and weaker, the bird's head drooped, and he sunk slowly down, and lay dead at their feet.

"It is a beautiful bird," said the traveler, "and these large white wings are worth a great deal of money. I will take them with me. You see now that a sword will be very useful."

So he cut off the wings of the dead swan with one blow, and carried them away with him.

They now kept on their journey over the mountains for many miles, till they at length reached a large city, with hundreds of towers, that shone in the sunshine like silver. In the middle of the city stood a splendid marble palace, roofed with pure red gold, in which lived the king.

John and his companion did not go into the town at once; they stopped at an inn outside the town, to change their clothes; for they wished to look their best when they walked through the streets. The landlord told them that the king was a very good man, who never did anyone harm; but as to his daughter, "Heaven help us—she was a wicked princess."

She was indeed a wicked princess. She had beauty enough—nobody could be prettier than she was; but what of that? She was a wicked witch and because of this many noble young princes had lost their lives. Anyone could ask to marry her, were he a prince or a beggar, it mattered not to her. She would ask him to guess three riddles which she had just thought of, and if he guessed right he could marry her, and be king over all the land when her father died; but if he could not guess these three riddles, then she ordered him to be hanged or to have his head cut off. The old king, her father, was very much grieved, but he could not prevent her from being so wicked, because he once said he would have nothing more to do with her lovers; she might do as she pleased. Each prince who came and tried the three guesses, so that he might marry the princess, had been unable to find them out, and had been hanged or had his head cut off. They had all been warned in time, and might have left her alone, if they would. The old king became at last so distressed that for a whole day every year he and his soldiers knelt and prayed that the princess might become good; but she kept on as wicked as ever. The old women who drank brandy would color it quite black before they drank it, to show how they mourned; and what more could they do?

"What a horrible princess!" said John, "she ought to be well whipped. If I were the old king, I would have her punished in some way."

Just then they heard the people outside shouting, "Hurrah!" and, looking out, they saw the princess passing by; and she was really so beautiful that everybody forgot her wickedness, and shouted "Hurrah!" Twelve lovely girls in white silk dresses, holding golden tulips in their hands, rode by her side on coalblack horses. The princess herself had a snow-white steed, decked with diamonds and rubies. Her dress was of cloth of gold, and the whip she held in her hand looked like a sunbeam. The golden crown on her head glittered like the stars of heaven, and her mantle was formed of thousands of butterflies' wings sewn together. Yet she herself was more beautiful than all.

When John saw her his face became as red as a drop of blood, and he could scarcely speak a word. The princess looked exactly like the beautiful lady with the golden crown, of whom he had dreamed on the night his father died. She looked to him so lovely that he could not help loving her.

"It could not be true," he thought, "that she was really a wicked witch, who ordered people to be hanged or beheaded, if they could not guess her thoughts. Everyone is allowed to go and ask her to marry, even the poorest beggar. I shall pay a visit to the palace," he said; "I must go, for I cannot help myself."

Then they all urged him not to go; for he would be sure to share the same fate as the rest. His fellow traveler also tried to keep him back, but John seemed quite sure of success. He brushed his shoes and his coat, washed his face and his hands, combed his soft flaxen hair, and then went out alone into the town, and walked to the palace.

"Come in," said the king, as John knocked at the door. John opened it, and the old king in a dressing gown and embroidered slippers came towards him. He had the crown on his head, carried his scepter in one hand, and the golden ball in the other. "Wait a bit," said he, and he placed the ball under his arm, so that he could offer the other hand to John; but when he found that John was another suitor, he began to cry so hard that both the scepter and the ball fell to the floor, and he was obliged to wipe his eyes with his dressing gown. Poor old king!

"Let her alone," he said; "you will fare as badly as all the others. Come, I will show you." Then he led him out into the princess's pleasure gardens, and there he saw a frightful sight. On every tree hung three or four kings' sons who had wooed the princess, but had not been able to guess the riddles she gave them. Their bones rattled in every breeze, so that the little birds never dared to stay in the garden. All the flowers were tied up to human bones instead of sticks, and human skulls in the flowerpots grinned horribly. It was a nice garden for a princess!

"Do you see all this?" said the old king; "your fate will be the same as those who are here; so do not go on. You really make me very unhappy—I take these things to heart so very much." John kissed the good old king's hand, and said he was sure it would be all right, for he was quite enchanted with the beautiful princess.

Then the princess herself came riding into the palace yard with all her ladies, and he wished her "Good morning." She looked wonderfully fair and lovely when she offered her hand to John, and he loved her more than ever. How could she be a wicked witch, as all the people said? He went with her into the hall, and the little pages offered them gingerbread nuts and sweetmeats, but the old king was so unhappy he could eat nothing, and besides, gingerbread nuts were too hard for him.

It was decided that John should come to the palace the next day, when the judges and the whole of the counselors would be there, to try if he could guess the first riddle. If he guessed right, he would have to come a second time; but if not, he would lose his life— and no one had ever been able to guess even one.

John was not at all anxious; on the contrary, he was very merry. He thought only of the beautiful princess, and believed that in some way he should have help, but how he knew not, and did not like to think about it; so he danced along the highroad as he went back to the inn where he had left his fellow traveler waiting for him. John could not keep from telling him how gracious the princess had been, and how beautiful she looked. He longed for the next day so much, that he might go to the palace and try his luck at guessing the riddles. But his comrade shook his head, and looked very mournful.

"I do so wish you to do well," said he; "we might have kept together much longer, and now I am likely to lose you; you poor dear John! I could shed tears, but I will not make you unhappy on the last night we may be together. We will be merry, really merry this evening; tomorrow, after you are gone, I shall be able to cry."

It was very quickly known among the people of the town that another suitor had come for the princess, and there was great sorrow. The theater was closed, the women who sold candy tied crepe round the sugar sticks, and the king and the priests were on their knees in the church. There was a great grief, for no one expected John to do better than those who had been suitors before.

In the evening John's comrade prepared a large bowl of punch, and said, "Now let us be merry, and drink to the health of the princess." But after drinking two glasses John became so sleepy that he could not possibly keep his eyes open, and fell fast asleep. Then his fellow traveler lifted him gently out of his chair, and laid him on the bed; and as soon as it was quite dark, he took the two large wings which he had cut from the dead swan, and tied them firmly to his own shoulders. Then he put into his pocket the largest of the three rods which he had got from the old woman who had fallen and broken her leg. After this he opened the window, and flew away over the town, straight towards the palace, and seated himself in a corner, under the very window which looked into the bedroom of the princess.

The town was perfectly still when the clocks struck a quarter to twelve. Presently the window opened, and the princess, who had large black wings to her shoulders, and a long white mantle, flew away over the city towards a high mountain. The fellow traveler, who had made himself invisible, so that she could not possibly see him, flew after her through

the air, and whipped the princess with his rod, so
that the blood came whenever he struck her. Ah, it
was a strange flight through the air! The wind
caught her mantle, so that it spread out on all sides,
like the large sail of a ship, and the moon shone
through it. "How it hails, to be sure!" said the
princess, at each blow she got from her pursuer's
rod; and it served her right to be whipped.

At last she reached the side of the mountain, and
knocked. The mountain opened with a noise like
the roll of thunder, and the princess went in. The
traveler followed her; no one could see him, as he
was quite invisible. They went through a long, wide
passage. A thousand gleaming spiders ran here and
there on the walls, causing them to glitter as if they
were on fire. They next reached a large hall built of
silver and gold. Large red and blue flowers shone
on the walls, looking like sunflowers in size, but no
one could dare to pluck them, for the stems were
hideous poisonous snakes, and the flowers were flames
of fire, darting out of their jaws. Shining glow-
worms covered the ceiling, and sky-blue bats flapped
their wings. Altogether the place had a frightful ap-
pearance. In the middle of the floor stood a throne
held up by four horses, whose harness had been made
by fiery-red spiders. The throne itself was made of
milk-white glass, and the cushions were little black
mice, each biting the other's tail. Over it hung a

canopy of rose-colored spider's webs, spotted with
the prettiest little green flies, which sparkled like
precious stones. On the throne sat an old magician
with a crown on his ugly head, and a scepter in his
hand. He kissed the princess on the forehead, seated
her by his side on the splendid throne, and then the
music began. Great black grasshoppers played the
mouth organ, and the owl struck herself on the body
instead of a drum. It was altogether a ridiculous
concert. Little black goblins with false lights in their
caps danced about the hall; but no one could see the
traveler, and he had placed himself just behind the
throne, where he could see and hear everything. The
courtiers who came in afterward looked noble and
grand, but anyone with common sense could see that
they really were only broomsticks, with cabbages for
heads. The magician had given them life, and dressed
them in embroidered robes. It did very well, as they
were only wanted for show. After there had been a
little dancing, the princess told the magician that she
had a new suitor, and asked him what she should
think of for the suitor to guess when he came to the
castle the next morning.

"Listen to what I say," said the magician; "you
must choose something very easy; he is less likely to
guess it then. Think of one of your shoes; he will
never guess that. Then cut his head off; and mind

you do not forget to bring his eyes with you tomorrow night, that I may eat them."

The princess curtsied low, and said she would not forget the eyes.

The magician then opened the mountain and she flew home again, but the traveler followed and flogged her so much with the rod, that she sighed quite deeply about the heavy hail storm, and made as much haste as she could to get back to her bedroom through the window.

The traveler then went back to the inn where John still slept, took off his wings and laid down on the bed, for he was very tired. Early in the morning John awoke, and when his fellow traveler got up, he said that he had had a very wonderful dream about the princess and her shoe, so he advised John to ask her if she had not thought of her shoe. Of course the traveler knew this from what the magician in the mountain had said.

"I may as well say that as anything else," said John. "Perhaps your dream may come true; still I will say good-by, for if I guess wrong I shall never see you again."

Then they kissed each other, and John went into the town and walked to the palace. The great hall was full of people, and the judges sat in armchairs, with eider down cushions to rest their heads upon, because they had so much to think of. The old king stood near, wiping his eyes with his white pocket handkerchief. When the princess came in she looked even more beautiful than she had the day before, and greeted everyone present most gracefully; but to John she gave her hand, and said, "Good morning to you."

Now came the time for John to guess what she was thinking of; and, oh, how kindly she looked at him as she spoke. But when he said the single word shoe, she turned as pale as a ghost; all her wisdom could not help her, for he had guessed rightly. Oh, how pleased the old king was! It was quite amusing to see how he capered about. All the people clapped their hands, both on his account and John's, who had guessed rightly the first time. His fellow traveler was glad also when he heard how successful John had been. But John folded his hands, and thanked God, who, he felt quite sure, would help him again; and he knew he had to guess twice more.

The evening passed pleasantly like the one preceding. While John slept, his companion flew behind the princess to the mountain, and flogged her even harder than before; this time he had taken two rods with him. No one saw him go in with her, and he heard all that was said. The princess this time was to think of a glove, and he told John as if he had again heard it in a dream.

So the next day he was able to guess correctly the second time, and it caused great rejoicing at the palace. The whole court jumped about as they had seen the king do the day before, but the princess lay on the sofa, and would not say a single word. All now depended upon John. If he only guessed rightly the third time, he would marry the princess, and reign over the kingdom after the death of the old king; but if he failed, he would lose his life, and the magician would have his beautiful blue eyes.

That evening John said his prayers and went to bed very early, and soon fell asleep calmly. But his companion tied on his wings to his shoulders, took three rods, and, with his sword at his side, flew to the palace. It was a very dark night, and so stormy that the tiles flew from the roofs of the houses, and the trees in the garden upon which the bones hung bent themselves like reeds before the wind. The lightning flashed, and the thunder rolled in one long peal all night. The window of the castle opened, and the princess flew out. She was pale as death, but she laughed at the storm as if it were not bad enough. Her white mantle fluttered in the wind like a large sail, and the traveler flogged her with the three rods till the blood trickled down, and at last she could scarcely fly; but at last they reached the mountain. "What a hailstorm!" she said, as she went in: "I have never been out in such weather as this."

"Yes, there may be too much of a good thing sometimes," said the magician.

Then the princess told him that John had guessed rightly the second time, and if he succeeded the next morning he would win, and she could never come to the mountain again, or practice magic as she had done, and so she was quite unhappy. "I will find out something for you to think of which he will never guess, unless he is a greater magician than myself. But now let us be merry."

Then he took the princess by both hands, and they danced with all the little goblins and Jack o'Lanterns in the room. The red spiders sprang here and there on the walls quite as merrily, and the flowers of fire appeared as if they were throwing out sparks. The owl beat the drum, the crickets whistled, and the grasshoppers played the mouth organ. It was a very ridiculous ball.

After they had danced enough, the princess was obliged to go home, for fear she should be missed at the palace. The magician offered to go with her, that they might be company to each other on the way. Then they flew away through the bad weather, and the traveler followed them, and broke his three rods across their shoulders. The magician had never been out in such a hailstorm as this. Just by the palace the magician stopped to wish the princess good-by and to whisper in her ear, "Tomorrow think of my head."

But the traveler heard it, and just as the princess slipped through the window into her bedroom, and the magician turned round to fly back to the mountain, he seized him by the long black beard, and with his saber cut off the wicked one's head just behind his shoulders, so that he could not even see who it was. He threw the body into the sea to the fishes, and after dipping the head into the water, he tied it up in a silk handkerchief, took it with him to the inn, and then went to bed.

The next morning he gave John the handkerchief, and told him not to untie it till the princess asked him what she was thinking of. There were so many people in the great hall of the palace that they stood as thick as radishes tied together in a bundle. The Council sat in their armchairs with the white cushions. The old king wore new robes, and the golden crown and scepter had been polished up so that he looked quite smart. But the princess was very pale, and wore a black dress as if she were going to a funeral.

"What have I thought of?" asked the princess, of John. At once he untied the handkerchief, and was himself quite frightened when he saw the head of the ugly magician. Everyone shuddered, for it was terrible to look at; but the princess sat like a statue, and could not speak a single word. At length she rose and gave John her hand, for he had indeed guessed rightly.

She looked at no one, but sighed deeply, and said, "You are my master now; this evening our marriage shall take place."

"I am very pleased to hear it," said the old King, "it is just what I wish."

Then all the people shouted "Hurrah!" The band played music in the street, the bells rang, and the cake-women took the back crepe off the sugar sticks. Everyone was happy. Three oxen, stuffed with ducks and chickens, were roasted whole in the market place, where everyone might help himself to a slice. The fountains spouted forth the most delicious wine, and whoever bought a penny loaf at the baker's got six large buns, full of raisins, as a present.

In the evening the whole town was lighted up. The soldiers fired off cannons, and the boys let off crackers. There was eating and drinking, dancing and jumping everywhere. In the palace, the highborn gentlemen and the beautiful ladies danced with each other, and they could be heard at a great distance singing the following song:

"Here are ladies, young and fair,
Dancing in the summer air;
Like to spinning wheels at play,
Pretty maidens dance away—
Dance the spring and summer through
Till the sole falls from your shoe."

But the princess was still bewitched, and she could not love John. His fellow traveler had thought of that, so he gave John three feathers out of the swan's wings, and a little bottle with a few drops in it. He told him to place a large bath full of water by the princess's bed, and put the feathers and the drops into it. Then, at the moment she was about to get into bed, he must give her a little push, so that she might fall into the water, and then dip her three times. This would take away the power of the magician, and she would love him very much.

John did all that his companion told him to do. The princess shrieked aloud when he dipped her under the water the first time, and struggled under his hands in the form of a great black swan with fiery eyes. As she rose the second time from the water, the swan had become white, with a black ring round its neck. John let the water close once more over the bird, and this time it changed into a most beautiful princess. She was more lovely even than before, and thanked him, while her eyes sparkled with tears, for having broken the spell of the magician.

The next day the king came with the whole court to wish them joy, and stayed till quite late. Last of all came the traveling companion; he had his staff in his hand and his knapsack on his back. John kissed him many times and told him he must not go, he must stay with him, for he was the cause of all his good fortune. But the traveler shook his head, and said gently and kindly, "No, my time is up now; I have

only paid my debt to you. Do you remember the
dead man whom the bad people wished to throw out
of his coffin? You gave all you had that he might
rest in his grave; I am that man." As he said this,
he vanished.

The wedding festival lasted a whole month. John
and his princess loved each other dearly, and the old
king lived to see many a happy day, when he took
their little children on his knees and let them play
with his scepter. And John was king over the whole
country.

The Real Princess ✍

THERE WAS once a Prince who wished to marry a princess, but she must be a real princess. So he traveled about the whole world to find such a one, but everywhere there was something in the way. Princesses there were plenty, but whether they were real princesses he could not be sure, for there was always something that did not seem quite right. So he came home again and was quite sad, for he wished so very much to have a real princess.

One night a terrific storm came on; it thundered and lightened, and the rain poured down dreadfully. There was then a knocking at the gate of the town, and the old King went to open it.

It was a princess who stood outside at the gate. And, good heavens! what a state she was in. The water ran down from her hair and her clothes, in at the toes of her shoes and out at the heels, but she said she was a real princess.

"Well, that we'll soon find out," the old Queen

thought; she said nothing, however, but went into the bedroom and having taken all the things off the bed, laid a small pea upon the slabs, upon which she heaped twenty mattresses, and then twenty eider down quilts upon the mattresses.

There the princess was to lie that night.

In the morning she was asked how she had slept.

"Oh, abominably, badly!" she answered. "I have scarcely closed my eyes the whole night. Heaven knows what there may have been in the bed! but I lay upon something hard, so that I am black and blue all over my body. It is quite dreadful."

It was plain, then, that she was a real princess, since she had felt the pea through the twenty mattresses and the twenty eider down quilts. No one could have so very fine a sense of feeling but a real Princess.

So the Prince married her, for he knew that now he had a real Princess; and the pea was placed in the royal museum, where it may still be seen if no one has taken it away.

Now, this is a true story.

The Bell ✑

I N the evening, at sunset, when golden clouds could just be seen among the chimney tops, a curious sound would be heard, first by one person, then by another; it was like a church bell, but it only lasted for a moment because of the noise of carts and the street cries.

"There is the evening bell," people would say; "the sun is setting."

Those who went outside the town where the houses were more scattered, each with its garden or little meadow, saw the evening star and heard the tones of the bell much better. It seemed as if the sound came from a church buried in silent, fragrant woods, and people looked that way, feeling quite peaceful.

Time passed, and still people said one to the other, "Can there be a church in the woods! that bell has such a wonderfully sweet sound; shall we go and look

at it closer?" The rich people drove and the poor
ones walked, but it was a very long way; when they
reached a group of willows which grew on the edge
of the wood, they sat down and looked up among
the long branches, thinking that they were really in
the heart of the forest. A candy man from the town
came out and pitched a tent there, and then another
candy man, and he hung a bell up over his tent. This
bell was tarred so as to stand the rain, and it had no
clapper. When people went home again they said
it had been so pretty, and that meant something more
than mere tea. Three people said that they had
walked right through the forest to the other side, and
that they had heard the same curious bell all the
time but that then it sounded as if it came from the
town.

One of them wrote a poem about it, and said that
it sounded like a mother's voice to a beloved child;
no melody could be sweeter than the chimes of this
bell.

The Emperor was told about it, and he promised
that anyone who really found where the sound came
from should have the title of "the world's bell-
ringer," even if there was no bell at all.

A great many went to the woods to earn an honest
penny, but only one of them brought home any kind
of news. No one had been far enough, not even he
himself, but he said that the sound of the bell came

from a very big owl in a hollow tree; it was a wise
owl, which kept on beating its head against a tree,
but whether the sound came from its head or from
the hollow tree he could not say. All the same he
was appointed "world's bell-ringer," and every year
he wrote a little paper about the owl, but nobody was
much the wiser for it.

Now on a Sunday the priest had preached a very
moving sermon; all the young people had been much
touched by it. It was a beautiful sunny day and
after church the young people walked out of the
town and they heard the sound of the unknown bell
more than usually loud coming from the wood. On
hearing it they all felt anxious to go further and see
it; all but three. The first of these had to go home
to try on her ball dress. The second was a poor boy,
who had borrowed his coat and boots of the landlord's son and he had to carry them back before night.

The third said that he had never been anywhere
without his mother, that he had always been a good
child and he meant to keep on so.

So these three did not go; the others trudged off.
The sun shone and the birds sang and the young people took each other by the hand and sang with them.
Soon two of the smallest ones got tired and they went
back to town; two little girls sat down and made
wreaths, so they did not go either. When the others
got to the willows where the candy men had their

tents they said, "Now, then, here we are; there is not any bell, it is only something people imagine!"

Just then a bell was heard in the wood, with its deep rich notes; and four or five of them decided after all to go further into the wood. The under-wood was so thick and close that it was quite hard to walk. The bushes grew almost too high, and brambles hung in long garlands from tree to tree, where the nightingales sang and the sunbeams played. It was lovely and peaceful, but there was no path for the girls, their clothes would have been torn to shreds. There were great boulders overgrown with many colored mosses, and fresh springs trickled among them with a curious little gurgling sound.

"Surely that cannot be the bell!" said one of the young people, as he lay down to listen.

"I must look into this." So he stayed behind and let the others go on.

They came to a little hut made of bark and branches, overhung by a crab apple tree, as if it wanted to shake all its bloom over the roof, which was covered with roses. The long sprays clustered round the gable, and on it hung a little bell. Could this be the one they sought? Yes, they were all agreed that it must be, except one; he said it was far too small and delicate to be heard so far away as they had heard it, and that the tones which moved all hearts were quite different from these. He who spoke was a king's son, and so the others said "that kind of fellow must always be wiser than anyone else."

So they let him go on alone, and as he went he still heard the little bell with which the others were so pleased, and now and then when the wind came from the direction of the candy men he could hear the children calling for tea.

But the deep-toned bell sounded above them all, and it seemed as if there was an organ playing with it, and the sounds came from the left, where the heart is placed.

There was a rustling among the bushes, and a little boy stood before the king's son; he had wooden shoes on, and such a small jacket that the sleeves did not cover his wrists. They knew each other, for he was the boy who had had to go back with the coat and the boots to the landlord's son. He had done this, changed back into his shabby clothes and wooden shoes, and then, drawn by the deep notes of the bell, had come to the wood again.

"Then we can go together," said the king's son.

But the poor boy in the wooden shoes was too bashful. He pulled down his short sleeves, and said he was afraid he could not walk quickly enough, besides he thought the bell ought to be looked for on the right, because that side looked the most beautiful.

"Then we shan't meet at all," said the king's son, nodding to the poor boy, who went into the thickest and darkest part of the wood, where the thorns tore his shabby clothes and scratched his face, hands and feet till they bled. The king's son got some good scratches too, but he at least had the sun shining upon his path. We are going to follow him, for he is a bright fellow.

"I must and will find the bell," said he, "if I have to go to the end of the world."

Some horrid monkeys sat up in the trees grinning and showing their teeth.

"Shall we throw nuts at him?" said they. "Shall we thrash him; he is a king's son."

But he went bravely on further and further into the wood, where the most beautiful flowers grew. There were white star-like lilies with red hearts, pale blue tulips which glistened in the sun, and apple trees on which the apples looked like great shining soap bubbles. You may fancy how these trees glittered in the sun. Round about were beautiful green meadows, where deer played under the spreading oaks and beeches. There were also great quiet lakes, where white swans swam about flapping their wings. The king's son often stopped and listened, for he sometimes fancied that the bell sounded from one of these lakes; but then again he felt sure that it was not there, but further in the wood.

Now the sun began to go down, and the clouds were fiery red; a great stillness came over the wood, and he sank upon his knees, sang his evening psalm, and said, "Never shall I find what I seek, now the

He had reached the same goal just as soon by his own road.

sun is going down, the night is coming on—the dark
night; perhaps I could catch one more glimpse of the
round, red sun before it sinks beneath the earth. I
will climb upon to those rocks; they are as high as
the trees."

He seized the roots and creepers, and climbed up
the slippery stones where the water-snakes wriggled
and the toads seemed to croak at him; but he got to
the top before the sun disappeared. Seen from this
height, oh, what splendor lay before him! The
ocean, the wide, beautiful ocean, its long waves roll-
ing toward the shore. The sun still stood like a great
shining altar, out there where sea and sky met.
Everything melted away into glowing colors; the
wood sang, the ocean sang, and his heart sang, with
them. All Nature was like a great holy church,
where trees and floating clouds were the pillars,
flowers and grass the woven carpet, and the heaven
itself a great dome. The red colors faded as the sun
went down, but millions of stars peeped out; they
were like many diamond lamps, and the king's son
spread out his arms towards heaven, sea and wood.
At that moment from the right-hand path came the
poor boy with the short sleeves and wooden shoes.
He had reached the same goal just as soon by his own
road. They ran toward each other and clasped each
other's hands in that great church, and above them
sounded the unseen holy bell.

The Storks ~

O<small>N</small> the last house in a little village stood a stork's nest. The Mother Stork sat in it with her four young ones, who stretched out their heads with the pointed black beaks, for their beaks had not yet turned red. A little way off stood the Father Stork, all alone on the ridge of the roof, quite upright and stiff; he had drawn up one of his legs, so as not to be quite idle while he stood guard. One would have thought he had been carved out of wood, so still did he stand. He thought, "It must look very grand, that my wife has a guard standing by her nest. They can't tell that it is her husband. They certainly think I have been ordered to stand here. That looks so grand!" And he went on standing on one leg.

Below in the street a whole crowd of children were playing; and when they caught sight of the storks, one of the boldest of the boys, and afterward all of them, sang the old verse about the storks:

147

"Stork, stork, fly away;
Stand not on one leg today.
Thy dear wife is in the nest,
Where she rocks her young to rest.

"The first he will be hanged,
The second will be hit,
The third he will be shot,
And the fourth put on the spit."

"Just hear what those boys are saying!" said the little stork children. "They say we're to be hanged and killed."

"You're not to care for that!" said the Mother Stork. "Don't listen to it, and then it won't matter."

But the boys went on singing, and pointed at the storks mockingly with their fingers; only one boy, whose name was Peter, declared that it was wrong to make fun of animals, and he would not join in it at all.

The Mother Stork comforted her children. "Don't you mind it at all," she said; "see how quiet your father stands, though it's only on one leg."

"We are very much afraid," said the young storks, and they drew their heads far back into the nest.

Now today, when the children came out again to play, and saw the storks, they sang their song:

"The first he will be hanged,
The second will be hit . . ."

"Shall we be hanged and beaten?" asked the young storks.

"No, certainly not," replied the mother. "You shall learn to fly; I'll train you; then we shall fly out into the meadows and pay a visit to the frogs; they will bow before us in the water, and sing 'Co-ax! co-ax!' and then we shall eat them up. That will be great fun.

"And what then?" asked the young storks.

"Then all the storks will come together, all that are here in the whole country, and the autumn training will begin; then one must fly well, for that is important, for whoever cannot fly properly will be killed by the general's beak; so take care and learn well when the training begins."

"But then we shall be killed, as the boys say—and only listen, now they're singing again."

"Listen to me, and not to them," said the Mother Stork. "After the great parade we shall fly away to the warm countries, far away from here, over mountains and forests. We shall fly to Egypt, where there are three great buildings of stone, which reach to a point and tower above the clouds; they are called pyramids, and are older than a stork can imagine. There is a river in that country which runs out of its bed, and then all the land is turned to mud. One walks about in the mud, and eats frogs."

"Oh!" cried all the young ones.

"Yes! It is glorious there! One does nothing all day long but eat; and while we are so comfortable over there, here there is not a green leaf on the trees; here it is so cold that the clouds freeze to pieces, and fall down in little white rags!"

It was the snow that she meant, but she could not explain it in any other way.

"And do the naughty boys freeze to pieces?" asked the young storks.

"No, they do not freeze to pieces; but they are not far from it, and must sit in the dark room and shiver. You, on the other hand, can fly about in foreign lands, where there are flowers, and the sun shines warm."

Now after some time, the nestlings had grown so large that they could stand upright in the nest and look far around; and the Father Stork came every day with delicious frogs, little snakes, and all kinds of stork dainties as he found them. Oh! it looked funny when he cut capers before them! He stretched his head quite back upon his tail, and clapped with his beak as if he had been a little clapper; and then he told them stories, all about the marshes.

"Listen! now you must learn to fly," said the Mother Stork one day; and all the four young ones had to go out on the ridge of the roof. Oh, how they tottered! How they balanced themselves with their wings, and yet they were nearly falling down.

"Only look at me," said the mother. "Thus you must hold your heads! Thus you must pitch your feet! One, two! one, two! That's what will help you on in the world."

Then she flew a little way, and the young ones made a little clumsy leap. Bump!—there they lay, for their bodies were too heavy.

"I will not fly!" said one of the young storks, and crept back into the nest; "I don't care about getting to the warm countries.

"Do you want to freeze to death here, when the winter comes? Are the boys to come and hang you, and singe you, and roast you? Now I'll call them."

"Oh, no!" cried the young stork, and hopped out onto the roof again like the rest.

On the third day they could really fly a little, and then they thought they could also rise and hover in the air. They tried it, but—bump!—down they tumbled, and they had to shoot their wings again quickly enough. Now the boys came into the street again, and sang their song:

"Stork, stork, fly away!"

"Shall we fly down and pick their eyes out?" asked the young storks.

"No," replied the mother, "let them alone. Only listen to me, that's far more important. One, two, three!—now we fly round to the right. One, two, three!—now to the left round the chimney. See, that was very good! The last kick with your feet was so neat that tomorrow you shall fly with me to the marsh. Several nice stork families go there with their young. Show them that mine are the nicest, and that you can start proudly; that looks well, and every one will praise you."

"But are we not to punish the rude boys?" asked the young storks.

"Let them scream as much as they like. You will fly up to the clouds, and get to the land of the pyramids, when they will have to shiver, and not have a green leaf or a sweet apple."

Among all the boys down in the street, the one who most often was singing the teasing song was he who had begun it, and he was quite a little boy. He could hardly be more than six years old. The young storks certainly thought he was a hundred, for he was much bigger than their mother and father; and how should they know how old children and grown-up people can be? "We will punish that boy," they said.

"We must first see how you behave at the grand parade," replied their mother. "If you get through badly, so that the general stabs you through the chest with his beak, the boys will be right, at least in one way. Let us see."

"Yes, you shall see!" cried the young storks; and
then they took great pains. They practiced every
day, and flew so neatly and so lightly that it was a
pleasure to see them.

Now the autumn came on; all the storks began to
come together, to fly away to the warm countries to
stay while it is winter here. That *was* a parade.
They had to fly over forests and villages, to show
how well they could do it, for it was a long journey
they had before them. The young storks did their
part so well that they as a mark, "Remarkably well,
with frogs and snakes." That was the highest mark,
and they might eat the frogs and snakes; and that is
what they did.

"Now we shall punish them!" said the young storks.

"Yes, certainly!" said the Mother Stork. "What
I have thought of will be the best. I know the pond
in which all the little babies lie till the stork comes
and brings them to their mothers. The pretty little
babies lie there and dream so sweetly as they never
dream afterward. All mothers are glad to have such
a child, and all children want to have a sister or a
brother. Now we will fly to the pond, and bring
one for each of the children who have not sung the
naughty song and laughed at the storks."

"But he who began to sing—that naughty ugly
boy!" screamed the young storks; "what shall we
do with him?"

"He shall be left with no little sister or brother and he will cry because he has been left out. But that good boy—you have not forgotten him, the one who said, 'It is wrong to laugh at animals!' for him we will bring a brother and a sister too. And as his name is Peter, all of you shall be called Peter too."

And it was done as she said; all the storks were named Peter, and so they are all called even now.

The Bottle Neck

Dᴏᴡɴ in a narrow crooked street among other poor houses, stood a very high and narrow one, built of lath and plaster; it was very tumble-down and shaky. Here lived poor people, but the attic looked the poorest of all. Outside the window in the sunshine hung a battered bird cage, which had not even got a drinking glass, but only the neck of a bottle turned upside down, with a cork at the bottom. An old lady stood at the window; she had just been hanging chickweed all over the cage in which a little linnet hopped about from perch to perch, singing as gaily as possible.

"Ah, you may well sing!" said the bottle neck; but of course it did not say it as we should say it, for a bottle neck cannot talk, but it thought it within itself, much as when we talk to ourselves. "Yes, you may well sing, you who have your legs whole. You should try what it is like to have lost the lower part of your body like me, and only to have a neck and

155

mouth, and that with a cork in it, such as I have, and you wouldn't sing much. I have nothing to make me sing, nor could I if I would. But it is a good thing that somebody is happy. I have had no end of adventures. I have been through fire and water, and down into the black earth, and higher up than most people, and now I hang in the sunshine outside a bird cage. It might be worth while to listen to my story, but I don't speak very loud about it, for I can't."

Then it told or thought out its story. It was a curious story; the little bird twittered away happily enough, and down in the street people walked and drove as usual, all bent upon their own concerns, thinking about them, or about nothing at all; but not so the bottle neck. It told about the hot smelting furnace in the factory, where it had been blown into life. It still remembered feeling quite warm, and looking into the roaring furnace, its birthplace, and how it wished to leap back into it. But little by little, as it cooled, it began to feel quite comfortable where it was. It was standing in a row with a whole regiment of brothers and sisters, all from the same furnace, but some were blown into champagne bottles, and others into beer bottles, which makes all the difference in their after life!

All the bottles were soon packed up and our bottle with them. It never dreamed then of ending its days as a bottle neck serving as a drinking glass for a bird;

but after all that is an honorable position, so one is
something after all. It first saw the light again, when
with its other friends it was unpacked in the wine
merchant's cellar. Then it lay empty, and felt curi-
ously flat, it missed something, but did not know
exactly what it was. Next it was filled with some
good strong wine, was corked and sealed, and last of
all it was labeled outside "first quality." This was
just as if it had passed first-class in an examination,
but of course the wine was really good and so was the
bottle.

At last one morning the bottle was bought by the
furrier's boy; he was sent for a bottle of the best wine.
It was packed up in the lunch basket together with
the ham, the cheese and the sausage; the basket also
held butter of the best, and fancy breads. The furrier's daughter packed it herself, she was quite young
and very pretty. She had laughing brown eyes, and a
smile on her lips; her hands were soft and delicate
and very white, yet not so white as her neck and
bosom. It was easy to see that she was one of the
town beauties, and she was not engaged yet. She held
the basket on her lap during the drive to the wood.
The neck of the bottle peeped out beyond the folds
of the tablecloth. There was red sealing wax on the
cork, and it looked straight up into the girl's face;
and it also looked at the young sailor who sat beside
her. He was a friend since she was a child, the son

of a painter. He had just passed his examination, and was to sail next day as mate on a long trip far away. There had been a good deal of talk about this journey during the packing, and while it was going on the eyes and the mouth of the pretty girl looked anything but happy. The two young people walked together in the wood, and talked to each other. What did they talk about? Well the bottle did not hear, for it was in the lunch basket. It was a very long time before it was taken out, but then it was plain that something pleasant had taken place. Everybody's eyes were glad, and the furrier's daughter was laughing, but she talked less than the others, and her cheeks glowed like two red roses.

Father took up the bottle and the corkscrew—it felt curious for the cork to be drawn from the bottle for the first time. The bottle neck never afterward forgot when the cork flew out with a "kloop" and it gurgled when the wine flowed out of it into the glasses.

"The health of our two young people," said father; and every glass was drained, while the young sailor kissed his lovely bride.

"Health and happiness!" said both the old people. The young man filled the glasses again and drank to the "homecoming and the wedding this day year." When the glasses were emptied, he took the bottle and held it up above his head. "You have shared my

Two little peasant boys came along, peering among the reeds.

happiness today, and you shall serve nobody else,"
saying which he threw it up into the air. The furrier's
daughter little thought she was ever to see it again.
It fell among the rushes by a little woodland lake.
The bottle neck remembered how it lay there thinking over what had happened. "I gave them wine,
and they gave me swamp water in return, but they
meant it well." It could no longer see the happy pair
or the joyous old people, but it could hear them talking and singing.

After a time two little peasant boys came along
peering among the reeds, where they saw the bottle
and took it away with them. At home in the forester's
cottage where they lived, their oldest brother, who
was a sailor, had been yesterday to take leave of them,
as he was starting on a long voyage. Mother was now
packing up a bundle of his things which father was
to take to the town in the evening, when he went to
see his son once more, and to take his mother's last
greeting. A little bottle had already been filled with
spiced brandy, and was just being put into the bundle
when the two boys came in with the other larger
bottle they had found. This one would hold so much
more than the little one, and this was all the better.
It was no longer red wine like the last which was put
into the bottle, but bitter drops; but these were good
too—for the stomach. The large new bottle was to

go and not the little one; so once more the bottle started on a new journey. It was taken on board the ship to Peter Jensen, and it was the very same ship in which the young mate was to sail. But the mate did not see the bottle, and even if he had he would not have known it, nor would he ever have thought that it was the one out of which they had drunk to his homecoming.

Whenever Peter Jensen brought it out, his shipmates called it, "the apothecary." It held good medicine, and cured all their complaints as long as there was a drop left in it. It was a very pleasant time, and the bottle used to sing whenever it was stroked with a cork, so they called it "Peter Jensen's lark."

A long time passed and it stood in a corner empty, when something happened. A storm rose, great waves dark and heavy poured over the vessel and tossed it up and down. The masts were broken and one heavy sea sprang a leak; the pumps would not work, and it was a pitch dark night. The ship sank, but at the last moment the young mate wrote upon a scrap of paper the name of his bride, his own, and that of the ship, put the paper into an empty bottle he saw, hammered in the cork, and threw it out into the boiling waters. He did not know that it was the very bottle from which he had poured the drink of

joy and hope for her and for himself. Now it swayed
up and down upon the waves with farewells and a
message of death.

The ship sank, and the crew with it, but the bottle
floated like a bird, for it had a heart in it you know—
a lover's letter. The sun rose and the sun set and
looked to the bottle just like the glowing furnace in
its earliest days, when it wanted to leap back again.
It went through calms and storms: it never struck
against any rock, nor was it ever followed by sharks;
it drifted about for more than a year and a day, first
toward the north and then toward the south, just as
the current drove it.

The written paper, the last word from the bridegroom to the bride, could only bring sorrow, if it ever
came into the right hands. But where were those
hands, the ones which had shone so white when they
spread the cloth upon the fresh grass in the green
woods on the happy day? Where was the furrier's
daughter? Nay, where was the land, and which land
lay nearest? All this the bottle knew not; it drifted
and drifted till at last it was sick of drifting about;
it had to drift till at last it reached land—a strange
land. It did not understand a word that was said; it
was not the language it knew, and one loses much if
one does not understand the language.

The bottle was picked up and looked at, the bit
of paper inside was turned and twisted, but they did

not understand what was written on it. They saw
that the bottle had been thrown overboard, and that
something about it was written on the paper, but what
it was, this was the strange part. So it was put into
the bottle again, and this was put into a large cupboard in a large room in a large house.

Every time a stranger came the slip of paper was
taken out turned and twisted, so that the writing which
was only in pencil became more and more faded. At
last one could not even make out the letters. The
bottle stood in the cupboard for another year, then
it was put into the lumber room, where it was soon
hidden with dust and spiders' webs; then it used to
think of the better days when it poured forth red
wine in the wood, and when it danced on the waves
and carried a secret, a letter, a farewell sigh within it.

Now it stood in the attic for twenty years, it might
have stood there longer, if the house had not been re-
built. The roof was torn off, the bottle was seen and
talked about, but it did not understand the language;
one does not learn that by standing in a lumber room,
even for twenty years. "If I had stayed downstairs,"
it thought, "I should have learned it fast enough!"

Now it was washed and thoroughly rinsed out, it
became quite clear, and it felt youthful again in its
old age. But the slip of paper had been washed away.

The bottle was filled with seed corn, a sort of thing
it knew nothing at all about. Then it was well corked

and wrapped up tightly, so that it could neither see the light of lantern or candle, for less the sun or the moon—and "one really ought to see something when one goes on a journey," thought the bottle. But it saw nothing, and at last it came to some harbor, and there it was unpacked.

"What trouble these foreigners have taken with it!" was said, "but I suppose it is cracked all the same." No, it was not cracked. The bottle understood every single word that was said, it was all spoken in the language it had heard at the furnace, at the wine merchant's, in the wood, and on board ship—the one and only good old language which it thoroughly understood. It had come home again to its own country, where it had a hearty welcome in the language. It nearly sprang out of the people's hands from very joy; it hardly noticed the cork being drawn. Then it was well shaken to empty it, and put away in the cellar to be kept, and also forgotten. There is no place like home, even if it be a cellar. It lay there comfortably for many years; then one day some people came down and took away all the bottles and it among them.

In the garden outside everything was very gay. There were lamps and paper lanterns like tulips. It was a clear and lovely evening; the stars shone brightly, and the slim new moon was just up. It was a beautiful sight for good eyes. Bottles were placed in the hedges, each with a lighted candle in it, and among them stood

our bottle too, the one we know, which was to end
its days as a bottle neck for a bird's drinking fountain.
Everything here appeared lovely to the bottle, for it
was once again in the green wood and taking part once
more in merrymaking and gaiety. It heard music and
singing once again, and the hum and buzz of many
people, especially from that corner of the garden
where the lanterns shone and the paper lamps gave
their colored light. The bottle was only placed in
one of the side walks, but even there it was happy.
There it stood holding its light; it was being of some
use as well as giving pleasure, and that was the right
thing—in such an hour one forgets all about the
twenty years passed in an attic—and it is good sometimes to forget.

A couple of persons passed close by it, arm in arm,
like the happy pair in the woods, the sailor and the
furrier's daughter. The bottle felt as if it were living
its life over again. The guests walked about in the
garden, and other people too, who had come to look
at them and at the sights. Among them there was an
old lady who had no father or mother, but plenty of
friends. She was thinking of the very same thing as
the bottle; of the green wood and of a young pair
very dear to her, as she herself was one of them. It
had been her happiest hour, and that one never forgets, however old one may be. But she did not know
the bottle, and it did not know her again; thus people

pass one another in the world—till one meets again like these two who were now in the same town.

The bottle was taken from the garden to the wine merchant's where it was again filled with wine and sold to a man who next Sunday was to go up in a balloon. A crowd of people came to look on; there was a band and much excitement. The bottle saw everything from a basket, where it lay in company with a living rabbit, which was very sad, for it knew it was being taken up to be sent down in a parachute. The bottle knew nothing at all about it; it only saw that the balloon was being stretched to a great size, and when it could not get any bigger it began to rise higher and higher, and to become very restless. The ropes which held it were then cut, and it went up with the man, basket, bottle and rabbit. There was a grand clashing of music, and the people shouted "Hurrah!"

"It is curious to go up into the air like this!" thought the bottle. "It's a new kind of sailing, and there can't be any danger of hitting anybody up here!"

Several thousands of persons watched the balloon, and among them the old lady. She stood by her open window, where the cage hung with the little linnet, which at that time had no drinking fountain, but had to content itself with a cup. A myrtle stood in a pot in the window, and it was moved a little to one side so as not to be knocked over when the old lady leaned

out to look at the balloon. She could see the man in
the balloon quite plainly when he let the rabbit down
in the parachute; then he drank the health of the
people, after which he threw the bottle high up into
the air. Little did she think that she had seen the
same bottle fly into the air above her and her lover
on that happy day in the woods in her youth. The
bottle had no time to think, it was so taken by surprise
at finding itself higher than it had ever been before.
The church steeples and housetops lay far, far below,
and the people looked quite tiny. The bottle sank
down faster than the rabbit, and on the way it turned
several somersaults in the air; it felt so youthful. But
not for long. What a journey it had! The sun shone
upon the bottle, and all the people watched its flight;
the balloon was already far away, and the bottle was
soon lost to sight too. It fell upon a roof, where it
was smashed to pieces, but the bits of glass did not
lie where they fell; they jumped and rolled till they
reached the yard, where they lay in still smaller bits;
only the neck was whole, and that might have been
cut off with a diamond.

"That would do very well for a bird's drinking
fountain!" said the man who lived in the basement;
but he had neither bird nor cage, and it would have
been too much trouble to get a bird and a cage just
because he had found a bottle neck which would do
for a drinking fountain. The old lady in the attic

might find a use for it, so the bottle neck found its
way up to her. It had a cork put into it, and what
had been the top became the bottom; fresh water was
put into it and it was hung outside the cage of the little
bird which sang so merrily.

"Yes, you may well sing!" was what the bottle neck
said; and it was looked upon as a very remarkable one
for it had been up in a balloon. There it hung now
as a drinking fountain, where it could hear the roll
and the rumble in the streets below, and it could also
hear the old lady talking in the room. She had an old
friend with her, and they were talking, not about the
bottle neck, but about the myrtle in the window.

"You must certainly not spend five shillings on a
bridal bouquet for your daughter," said the old lady.
"I will give you a beauty covered with blossom. Do
you see how beautifully my myrtle is blooming. Why
it is a cutting from the plant you gave me; the one I
was to have had for my bouquet when the year was
out—the day which never came! Before then the
eyes which would have cared for me were closed.
He sleeps sweetly in the depths of the ocean—my
beloved! The tree grew old, but I grew older, and
when it drooped I took the last fresh branch and
planted it in the earth where it has grown to such a big
plant. So it will take part in a wedding after all, and
furnish a bouquet for your daughter!"

There were tears in the old lady's eyes as she spoke

THE BOTTLE NECK   169

of the beloved of her youth. She thought about the toasts which had been drunk, and about the first kiss— but of these she did not speak.

Of all the thoughts that came into her mind, this one never came, that just outside her window was something from those days, the neck of the bottle out of which the cork came with a pop when it was drawn on that happy day. The bottle neck did not know her either, in fact it was not listening to her, perhaps, because it was only thinking about itself.

Thumbelisa ❧

THERE was once a woman who wanted very much to have a wee little child, but had no idea whatever where she could find one. So she went to an old witch and said to her:

"I do so wish to have a little child; will you tell me where I can get one?"

"We'll soon arrange that!" said the witch. "Here is a barleycorn; it is not at all the sort which grows in the farmer's fields, or that fowls are given to eat. Put it in a flowerpot and you'll see something, I promise you."

"Thank you," said the woman, and she gave the witch twelve silver pennies, went home, and planted the barleycorn. At once a beautiful flower grew up which looked just like a tulip, but the leaves were all folded tightly together as if it were still budding.

"That's a pretty flower!" said the woman, and she kissed the lovely red and yellow petals. At that very moment the flower gave a loud crack and opened. It

170

was a real tulip, anyone could see that, but right in the middle of the flower sat a wee little girl, pretty and dainty. She was only as long as a thumb, so they called her Thumbelisa.

She was given a splendidly polished walnut shell for her cradle, she lay upon blue violet leaves, and had a rose leaf for her coverlet. There she slept at night, but in the daytime she played on the table, where the woman put a plate filled with a wreath of flowers with their stalks in the water; here a large tulip leaf floated, and on this leaf Thumbelisa used to sail from one end of the plate to the other; she had two white horse-hairs to row with. It was such a pretty sight! She could sing too, nicely and softly; never had the like been heard before.

One night, as she lay in her pretty cradle, an ugly old toad came hopping through a broken pane in the window. The toad was big and wet, and it hopped right onto the table where Thumbelisa lay sleeping beneath the red rose leaf.

"She would make a very nice wife for my son," said the toad, and with that she took up the walnut shell in which Thumbelisa lay and hopped away through the broken pane out into the garden. A broad river ran there, but close by the bank it was all swampy and muddy, and there the toad and her son lived together. Ugh! he, too, was nasty and ugly, like his mother.

"Koax-koax-brekke-ke-kex!" that was all he could say when he saw the pretty little girl in the walnut shell.

"Don't chatter so loudly or you'll wake her!" said the old toad; "she could give us the slip even now, for she is as light as swan's down. We'll put her out in the river, on one of the broad water lily leaves; she is so light and little that it will be quite an island to her. She can't get away from there while we are getting the room under the mud ready, where you are to live and keep house."

Out in the river grew many clumps of water lilies with broad, green leaves, that looked as if they were floating on the water; the leaf which was farthest out was also the largest; the old toad swam out to it, and placed Thumbelisa, nutshell and all, on top of it.

The poor little child awoke quite early in the morning, and when she saw where she was, she began to cry bitterly, for there was water on every side of the big green leaf, and she could not get ashore anyhow. The old toad was busy down in the mud, decorating her room with rushes and yellow sedges, for she wanted her new daughter-in-law to find it nice and pretty. After that she swam out with her ugly son to the leaf where Thumbelisa sat; they wanted to fetch away her pretty bed, as it was to be put into the chamber before the bride herself went there.

The old toad bowed low in the water and said, "Let

me introduce my son; he is to be your husband, and you will live together happily down in the mud."

"Koax-koax-brekke-ke-kex!" was all the son could say for himself.

So they took the pretty little cradle and swam away with it; but Thumbelisa sat alone on the green leaf and cried, for she did not want to live in the toad's house, nor to have her ugly son for a husband. Now, the little fishes who were swimming in the water had seen the toad and heard what she said, and they stuck their heads up to see the little girl. And as soon as they caught sight of her they thought her so pretty that they were quite angry at the idea of her going to live with the ugly toad. No, that should never be. So they swam around the green stem of the lily leaf below the water and gnawed it quite through. The leaf floated away down the river with Thumbelisa— far, far away, where the toad could not come.

Thumbelisa sailed past many places and the little birds in the bushes looked at her and sang, "What a sweet little girl!" On floated the leaf, farther and farther away, and thus little Thumbelisa went on her travels.

A pretty little white butterfly hovered over her, and at last it settled on the leaf, for it had taken quite a fancy to Thumbelisa. She was happy, for now the toad could not get at her, and as she sailed along the sun shone on the water like glistening gold and everything was very pretty. She took off her girdle and tied one end of it round the butterfly and the other end she fastened to the leaf; so now it floated along more quickly than ever.

Presently a big Maybug came flying along; he caught sight of her and instantly put his claw round her dainty waist and flew up into a tree with her. But the green leaf went sailing down the river and the butterfly with it, for he was fastened to the leaf and could not get away.

Gracious! how frightened, to be sure, was poor little Thumbelisa when the Maybug flew up into the tree with her. But she was anxious most of all about the poor white butterfly which she had tied fast to the leaf; if he could not get loose, he must surely starve to death! But the bug did not trouble himself about that at all. He sat down with her on the largest green leaf in the tree, gave her some honey from the flowers to eat, and told her that she was very pretty, although she did not look a bit like a Maybug.

After that the other Maybugs who lived in the tree came and paid them a visit; they looked at Thumbelisa, and shrugged their feelers and said, "Why she has only two legs; what a fright she looks!" "She has no feelers at all," they went on, "just look how slender her waist is! Fie! she looks just like a lady! How ugly she is!"

All the bugs said this, and yet Thumbelisa was

pretty after all. The Maybug who had run off with
her thought so too, but as all the others said she was
ugly, he got at last to believe she really was so, and
would have nothing more to do with her; she might
go where she liked, he said.

They flew down from the tree with her and placed
her on a daisy; there she sat and cried because she was
so ugly that even the Maybugs would have nothing to
do with her. And yet she was the loveliest little thing
you can imagine, as fine and delicate as the most
beautiful rose leaf.

All through the summer poor Thumbelisa lived
alone in the woods. She wove herself a bed of grass
stalks and hung it up under a large leaf so that the
rain could not fall upon her; she gathered honey from
the flowers for her food, and drank the dew which
lay fresh every morning on the leaves. Thus summer
and autumn passed away; but now winter had come,
the long, cold winter. All the birds that had sung so
prettily flew away, the flowers withered, the trees shed
their leaves, the large leaf she had lived under shrivelled
up and became a yellow, withered stalk, and she felt
horribly cold, for her clothes were in rags and she
herself was so little and delicate that she was likely to
freeze to death. Poor little Thumbelisa! And now
it began to snow, and every snowflake which fell upon
her was just as if one were to cast a whole spadeful
of snow upon one of us, for we are big and she was

no longer than a thumb. She wrapped herself up in
a withered leaf, but it did not warm her at all, and she
shivered with cold.

Close to the wood was a large cornfield, but the
corn had long since been cut and carried away; only
the bare, dry stubble stood up on the frozen ground.
To her indeed it was just like another great wood; oh,
how she shivered as she went through it! And thus
she came to the field mouse's door. It was a little
hole right under the stubble. There lived the field
mouse, quite warm and cosy; she had a whole room
full of corn, and a nice kitchen and pantry. Poor
Thumbelisa stood outside the door, like a beggar girl,
and begged for a little barleycorn, for she had not had
anything to eat for two days.

"You poor little creature!" said the field mouse,
for it was a kind-hearted field mouse; "come into my
warm room and eat with me!"

Afterwards she liked Thumbelisa so much that she
said, "You are quite welcome to stay with me all the
winter. But you must keep my room nice and clean
and tell me stories, for I am very fond of stories."

Thumbelisa did all the good old mouse required of
her, and had a very nice time of it.

"We shall soon be having a visitor," said the field
mouse one day; "my neighbor always visits me once
a week. He has a better house even than I, for he has
large halls and goes about in a beautiful black fur coat.

If only you could have him for a husband, you would be well cared for, but, I am sorry to say, he is blind. Now mind, tell him the very prettiest stories you know."

But Thumbelisa did not trouble her head about it at all, for she knew who the neighbor was—he was only a mole. So he came and paid them a visit in his fur coat; he was very rich and wise, said the field mouse, his house was ten times as large as hers; but he could not endure the sun and the pretty flowers; having never seen them, he did not know how beautiful they are.

Thumbelisa had to sing to him, and she sang "Fly Away, Maybug!" and "The Blackcap Trips the Meadow Along." The mole fell in love with her because of her sweet voice, but he said nothing at the time, for he was a very careful person.

He had dug himself a long passage under the earth from his own house to theirs, and he told the field mouse and Thumbelisa they might walk in it whenever they liked. At the same time he told them not to be frightened at the dead bird which lay in the passage; it was a whole bird with feathers and beak complete, which certainly must have died quite lately, when the winter began, and had been buried just where he was making his passage.

The mole took a piece of torchwood in his mouth, for it shines like fire in the dark, and went in front

to light them through the long, dark passage. When
they came to the dead bird, the mole put his broad
nose through the earth above till there was a large
hole. Through this the light shone on the body of a
dead swallow, with its pretty wings folded down to
its sides, and its head and legs drawn in beneath its
feathers; the poor bird had certainly died of cold.

Thumbelisa was very sorry for it, she was fond of
all little birds; had they not sung and twittered for
her so prettily all through the summer? But the mole
gave a kick at it with his short legs and said, "It will
chirp no more now. How miserable it must be to
be born a little bird! Thank Heaven, none of my
children will be *that!* Birds like that have nothing
in the world but their 'Kwee-wit! Kwee-wit!' and
they must starve to death in the winter, stupid things!"

"You may well say that, sensible creature as you
are," answered the field mouse. "What has a bird to
show for itself when the winter comes, for all its
'Kwee-witting'? It must starve and freeze to death!
very pretty, I daresay!"

Thumbelisa said nothing, but when the other two
had turned their backs on the dead bird, she bent down
over it, brushed aside the feathers which lay over its
head, and kissed its closed eyes. "Perhaps it was this
very one which sang so prettily to me in the summer,"
she thought; "what joy it gave me, the lovely, darling
bird!"

The mole now stopped up the hole through which the daylight shone and led the ladies home. But at night Thumbelisa could not sleep, so she rose from her bed, wove a large and pretty rug of hay, and took it down with her and spread it round the dead bird, laying some soft wool, which she had found in the field mouse's room, at the sides of the bird, that it might lie warm on the cold earth.

"Good-by, you pretty little bird!" said she, "good-by, and thank you for your pretty songs in the summertime, when all the trees were green and the sun shone so warmly upon us!"

Then she laid her head on the bird's breast, but was very much startled, for it was just as if something inside was going "Thump! thump!" It was the bird's heart. The bird was not really dead, and when the warmth stole over it, it came back to life. In the fall the swallows fly away to warmer lands, but if one is late and gets left behind, it gets so cold that it falls down as if dead, and the cold snow comes and buries it.

Thumbelisa trembled, so frightened was she, for really the bird was a big creature, much bigger than herself; but she tried to be brave, wrapped the cotton wool more closely round the poor swallow, and brought a leaf, which had served her as a coverlet, and put it over the bird's head.

The following night she again crept down to it, and there it was quite alive, but so weak that it could

only open its eye for a second and look at Thumbelisa,
who stood there with a little piece of torchwood in
her hand, for she had no other light.

"Many thanks, you pretty little child!" said the
sick swallow. "I am warm now. I shall soon get back
my strength, and be able to fly away to the warm
sunshine."

"Oh, not yet!" said she, "it is so cold outside, it is
snowing and freezing! Keep in your warm bed, and
I will nurse you!" She brought the swallow water
in a leaf, and when it had drunk it told her how it had
torn one of its wings on a thorn bush, and so could not
fly so strongly as the other swallows, when they flew
away to the warm lands. Then it had fallen to the
ground, but it could not remember anything more,
and did not know in the least how it had got there.

The swallow stayed the whole winter, and Thumbelisa was kind to it and loved it very much. Neither
the mole nor the field mouse was told a word about it,
for Thumbelisa knew they did not like birds.

As soon as the spring came and the sun had warmed
the earth, the swallow said good-by to Thumbelisa,
who opened the hole which the mole had made in
the ground. The sun then shone in gloriously, and
the swallow asked if she would not go with him; she
could sit on his back and they would fly far out into
the greenwood. But Thumbelisa knew that it would
grieve the old field mouse if she left her like that.

"No, I cannot come," said Thumbelisa.

"Good-by, good-by! you good, pretty little girl!" said the swallow, and flew out into the warm sunshine. Thumbelisa looked after it, and the tears came to her eyes, for she dearly loved the swallow.

"Kwee-wit! Kwee-wit!" sang the bird, and flew away into the greenwood. Thumbelisa was very sorrowful. She could not get leave anyhow to go into the warm sunshine; the corn which had been sown in the field over the field mouse's house had grown high in the air, and seemed like a thick wood to the poor little girl who was only as long as a thumb.

"This summer you must sew away at some new clothes," said the field mouse, for by this time their neighbor, the tiresome mole, had made up his mind that he wanted her to be his wife. "You must have both linen and woolen in your chest, for when you become the mole's wife you must sit down in the best and lie down in the best too."

So Thumbelisa had to spin away and the field mouse hired four spiders to weave for her night and day. Every evening the mole paid them a visit, and he always talked about the same thing, and said that when the summer came to an end the sun would not be so hot. Yes, and when the summer was over he would marry Thumbelisa; but she did not like that at all, for she could not bear the tiresome mole.

Every morning when the sun rose, and every evening when it set, she crept out-of-doors, and when the wind parted the tops of the corn, so that she could see the blue sky, she thought how beautiful it was in the light, and wished for the dear swallow once more. But it never came back; it must certainly have flown far away into the greenwood.

When fall came Thumbelisa's clothes were quite ready.

"In four weeks you shall be married," said the field mouse. But Thumbelisa began to cry, and said that she could not marry the tiresome mole.

"Fiddlesticks!" said the field mouse; "don't be obstinate, or I shall bite you with my white teeth. Such a handsome husband as you're going to have too! what more do you want? The queen herself has not the like of his black fur coat. He has food in plenty, too, in both kitchen and cellar. Be thankful for such a husband, say I!"

And so they were to be married. The mole had already come to fetch Thumbelisa away; she was to live with him deep down in the ground, and never come up into the warm sunlight at all, for he could not bear it. The poor child was so sad, but she got leave to bid the beautiful sun farewell, for while she had lived with the field mouse she had always been allowed to look at the sun from the door anyhow.

"Good-by, dear, golden sun!" she said, and stretched her arms high in the air, even going a little

way beyond the field mouse's door, for the corn had
been reaped, and only dry stubble stood there now.
"Good-by, good-by!" cried she, and threw her tiny
arms round a little scarlet flower that grew there.
"Give my love to the dear swallow if you ever see
him!"

"Kwee-wit! Kwee-wit!" sounded at that very
moment high above her head. She looked up. It
was the swallow just flying by. As soon as he saw
Thumbelisa he was delighted. She told him how she
did not want to have the blind mole for a husband,
and to live with him deep down under the ground
where the sun never shone. She could not keep back
her tears as she told him.

"The cold winter is coming now," said the swallow; "I am going to fly far away to the warm lands.
Will you come with me? You can sit upon my back.
You have only to tie yourself fast on with your girdle,
and then we will fly away from the ugly mole and his
dark room, high over the mountains to the warm lands
where the sun shines lovelier than here, and where
there is always summer. Do, pray, fly away with me,
you sweet little Thumbelisa, who saved my life when
I lay frozen in the dark earthy cellar!"

"Yes, I'll go with you," said Thumbelisa gladly.
She sat on the bird's back, her feet resting on its outspread wings, tied her belt fast to one of its strongest
feathers, and then the swallow flew high into the air,

over wood and over sea, and high up over the big mountains where snow always lies. Thumbelisa was almost frozen in the cold air, but she crept right in under the bird's warm feathers, only peeping out now and then to see all the beautiful things beneath her.

At last they came to the warm lands. There the sun shone much more brightly, the sky was twice as high, and in hedge and field grew the loveliest green and blue grapes. In the woods hung lemons and oranges, there was the smell of balsam and myrtle, and along the roads ran lovely children playing with large speckled butterflies. But the swallow flew still farther, and everything became lovelier and grander. Beneath stately green trees near a blue lake stood a white marble palace from the olden times. Vine tendrils twined up and around the high pillars, and at the very top were a number of swallow nests; in one of those lived the swallow who had carried Thumbelisa.

"Here is my house," said the swallow, "but please choose one of the most splendid of the flowers that grow, and I'll put you there and you shall have as happy a time as you can desire.

"Oh, that will be lovely!" cried she, clapping her tiny hands.

On the ground lay a large white marble column which had fallen and broken into three pieces, and between them grew the loveliest white flowers. The

swallow flew down with Thumbelisa and placed her
on one of the broad leaves; but how surprised was she
when she saw a little elf sitting in the very center
of the flower! He had on his head a tiny gold crown
and bright wings on his shoulders, and he was scarcely
any bigger than Thumbelisa. He was the elf of the
flower. In every flower there lived some such little
man or woman, but he was the King of all.

"How handsome he is!" whispered Thumbelisa to
the swallow.

The little prince was quite frightened at the swallow, for to him it was a giant bird, but when he saw
Thumbelisa he was delighted; she was the very prettiest
girl he had ever seen. He took his gold crown from
his head and put it on hers, asking her name and begging her to be his wife, for then she would be the
Queen of the flowers!

Now, here was someone like a husband, and very
different from the son of a toad, or a mole in his
black fur coat. Soon she said "Yes" to the pretty
prince, and from every flower came out a lord or a
lady elf, all so graceful that she was happy to see
them. At the wedding everyone brought Thumbelisa
a present, but the best of all was a pair of pretty
wings from a large white fly; they were fastened
onto Thumbelisa's back, so that she could fly from
flower to flower. There was a great merrymaking,
and the swallow sat overhead in his nest and sang

to them as well as he could, but at heart he was sorry, for he loved Thumbelisa, and he would have liked to be with her always.

"Good-by, good-by!" sang the swallow, a little later, and flew away again from the warm land—far, far away back to Denmark. There it has a little nest over the window of the man who tells fairy stories, and it sang to him, "Kwee-wit! Kwee-wit!" And that is how we got this story.

Old Shut-Eye (Ole-Luk-Oie) ❧

THERE's nobody in the whole world who knows so many stories as Ole-Luk-Oie He can tell capital histories. Toward evening, when the children, still sitting round the table as good as possible, or upon their little stools, Ole-Luk-Oie comes. He comes up the stairs quite softly, for he walks in his socks: he opens the door noiselessly, and *whisk!* he squirts sweet milk in the children's eyes, a small, small stream, but enough to keep them from keeping their eyes open; and thus they cannot see him. He creeps just among them, and blows softly upon their necks, and this makes their heads heavy. Yes, but it doesn't hurt them, for Ole-Luk-Oie is very fond of the children; he only wants them to be quiet, and that they are not until they are taken to bed; they are to be quiet in order that he may tell them stories.

When the children sleep, Ole-Luk-Oie sits down upon their bed. He is well dressed; his coat is of silk, but one cannot say of what color, for it shines red, green, and blue, according as he turns. Under each arm he carries an umbrella; the one with pictures on it he spreads over the good children, and then they dream all night the most glorious stories; but on his other umbrella nothing at all is painted: this he spreads over the naughty children, and these sleep in a dull way, and when they awake in the morning they have not dreamed of anything.

Now we shall hear how Ole-Luk-Oie, every evening through one whole week, came to a little boy named Hjalmar, and what he told him. There are seven stories, for there are seven days in the week.

MONDAY

"Listen," said Ole-Luk-Oie in the evening, when he had put Hjalmar to bed; "now I'll clear up the room."

And all the flowers in the flowerpots became great trees, stretching out their long branches under the ceiling of the room and along the walls, so that the whole room looked just like a beautiful bower; and all the twigs were covered with flowers, and each flower was more beautiful than a rose, and smelled so sweet that one wanted to eat it—it was sweeter than jam. The fruit gleamed like gold, and there were cakes bursting with raisins. It was most beautiful. But at the same time a terrible wail sounded

from the table drawer, where Hjalmar's schoolbook
lay.

"Whatever can that be?" said Ole-Luk-Oie; and he
went to the table and opened the drawer. It was the
slate, which was having a fit, for a wrong number
had got into the sum, so that it was nearly falling in
pieces; the slate pencil tugged and jumped at its string,
as if it had been a little dog who wanted to help the
sum; but he could not. And thus there was great
howling in Hjalmar's copybook; it was quite terrible
to hear. On each page the great letters stood in a row,
one beneath the other, and each with a little one at its
side—that was the copy. Next to these were a few
more letters which thought they looked just like the
first—these Hjalmar had written, but they lay down
just as if they had tumbled over the pencil lines on
which they were to stand.

"See, this is how you should hold yourself," said
the copy. "Look, sloping in this way, with a powerful swing!"

"Oh, we shall be very glad to do that," replied
Hjalmar's letters, "but we cannot; we are too weak."

"Then you must take medicine," said Ole-Luk-Oie.

"Oh, no," cried they; and at once they stood up
so gracefully that it was beautiful to behold.

"Yes, now we cannot tell any stories," said Ole-
Luk-Oie; "now I must exercise them. One, two!

one, two!" and thus he exercised the letters; and they stood quite slender, and as beautiful as any copy can be. But when Ole-Luk-Oie went away, and Hjalmar looked at them next morning, they were as weak and miserable as ever.

TUESDAY

As soon as Hjalmar was in bed, Ole-Luk-Oie touched all the furniture in the bedroom with his little magic wand, and at once the pieces began to talk together, and each one spoke of itself.

Over the chest of drawers hung a great picture in a gilt frame. One saw in it large old trees, flowers in the grass, and a broad river which flowed round about a forest, past many castles, and far out into the wide ocean.

Ole-Luk-Oie touched the painting with his magic wand, and the birds in it began to sing, the branches of the trees stirred, and the clouds began to move across it; one could see their shadows glide over the landscape.

Now Ole-Luk-Oie lifted little Hjalmar up to the frame, and put the boy's feet into the picture, just in the high grass; and there he stood and the sun shone upon him through the branches of the trees. He ran to the water, and seated himself in a little boat which lay there; it was painted red and white; the sails gleamed like silver, and six swans, each with a gold circle round its neck and a bright blue star on its fore-head, drew the boat past the great wood, where the trees tell of robbers and witches, and the flowers tell of the graceful little elves, and of what the butterflies have told them.

Gorgeous fishes, with scales like silver and gold, swam after their boat; sometimes they gave a spring, so that they splashed in the water; and birds, blue and red, little and great, flew after them in two long rows; the gnats danced, and the Maybugs said, "Boom! boom!" They all wanted to follow Hjalmar, and each one had a story to tell.

That was a happy voyage. Sometimes the forest was thick and dark, sometimes like a glorious garden full of sunlight and flowers; and there were great palaces of glass and marble; on the balconies stood princesses, and these were all little girls whom Hjalmar knew well—he had already played with them. Each one stretched forth her hand, and held out the prettiest sugar heart which ever a cake woman could sell; and Hjalmar took hold of each sugar heart as he passed by, and the princess held fast, so that each of them got a piece—she the smaller share and Hjalmar the larger. At each palace little princes stood guard. They shouldered golden swords, and caused raisins and tin soldiers to shower down; one could see that they were real princes. Sometimes Hjalmar sailed through for-ests, sometimes through halls or through the midst of

a town. He also came to the town where his nurse
lived, who had always been so kind to him; and she
nodded and beckoned, and sang the pretty verse she
had made herself and had sent to Hjalmar:

"I've loved thee, and kissed thee, Hjalmar, dear boy;
  I've watched thee waking and sleeping:
May the good Lord guard thee in sorrow, in joy,
  And have thee in His keeping."

And all the birds sang too, the flowers danced on
their stalks, and the old trees nodded, just as if Ole-
Luk-Oie had been telling stories to *them*.

WEDNESDAY

How the rain was streaming down outside! Hjalmar could hear it in his sleep, and when Ole-Luk-Oie
opened a window, the water stood quite up to the
windowsill; there was quite a lake outside, and a
noble ship lay close by the house.

"If thou wilt sail with me, little Hjalmar," said Ole-
Luk-Oie, "thou canst voyage tonight to foreign climes,
and be back again tomorrow."

And Hjalmar suddenly stood in his Sunday clothes
upon the glorious ship, and at once the weather became fine, and they sailed through the streets, and
steered round by the church, and now everything was
one great, wild ocean. They sailed on until the land
was no longer to be seen, and they saw a number of
storks, who also came from their home, and were

That was a happy voyage.

traveling toward the hot countries; these storks flew in a row, one behind the other, and they had already flown far—far! One of them was so tired that his wings would scarcely carry him farther; he was the very last in the row, and soon stayed a great way behind the rest; at last he sank, with outspread wings, deeper and deeper; he gave a few more strokes with his wings, but it was of no use; now he touched the rigging of the ship with his feet, then he glided down from the sail, and—bump!—he stood upon the deck.

Now the cabin boy took him and put him into the hen coop with the fowls, ducks, and turkeys. The poor stork stood among them embarrassed.

"Just look at the fellow!" said all the fowls.

And the turkey cock swelled himself up as much as ever he could, and asked the stork who he was; and the ducks walked backward and quacked to each other, "Quackery! quackery!"

And the stork told them of hot Africa, of the pyramids, and of the ostrich which runs like a wild horse through the desert; but the ducks did not understand what he said, and they said to one another,

"We all think that he's stupid."

"Yes, certainly he's stupid," said the turkey cock; and he gobbled.

Then the stork kept quite still, and thought of his Africa.

"Those are wonderful thin legs of yours," said the

turkey cock. "Pray, how much do they cost a yard?"

"Quack! quack! qua-a-ck!" grinned all the ducks; but the stork pretended not to hear it at all.

"You may just as well laugh, too," said the turkey cock to him, "for that was very wittily said. Or was it, perhaps, too high for you? Yes, yes, he isn't very bright. Let us keep on being interesting among ourselves."

And then he gobbled, and the ducks quacked, "Gick! gack! gick! gack!" It was terrible how they made fun among themselves.

But Hjalmar went to the hen coop, opened the back door, and called to the stork; and the stork hopped out to him on to the deck. Now he was quite rested, and it seemed as if he nodded at Hjalmar, to thank him. Then he spread his wings, and flew away to the warm countries; but the fowls clucked, and the ducks quacked, and the turkey cock became fiery red in the face.

"Tomorrow we shall make songs of you," said Hjalmar; and so saying he awoke, and was lying in his own little bed. It was a wonderful journey that Ole-Luk-Oie had caused him to take that night.

THURSDAY

"I tell you what," said Ole-Luk-Oie, "you must not be frightened. Here you shall see a little mouse," and he held out his hand with the pretty little crea-

ture in it. "It has come to invite you to a wedding.
There are two little mice here who are going to be
married tonight. They live under the floor of your
mother's storecloset, which is said to be a charming
home!"

"But how can I get through the little mousehole
in the floor?" asked Hjalmar.

"Let me manage that," said Ole-Luk-Oie. "I will
make you small."

And he touched Hjalmar with his magic wand, and
the boy began to shrink and shrink and shrink, until
he was not so long as a finger.

"Now you may borrow the uniform of a tin soldier. I think it would fit you, and it looks well to
wear a uniform when one is in society."

"Yes, certainly," said Hjalmar.

And in a moment he was dressed like the smartest
of tin soldiers.

"Will your honor not be kind enough to take a
seat in your mamma's thimble?" asked the mouse.
"Then I shall have the pleasure of drawing you."

"Will the young lady really take so much trouble?"
cried Hjalmar.

And thus they drove to the mouse's wedding. First
they came into a long passage beneath the boards,
which was only just so high that they could drive
through it in the thimble; and the whole passage was
lit up with rotten wood.

"Is there not a delicious smell here?" observed the mouse. "The entire road has been greased with bacon rinds, and there can be nothing more pretty."

Now they came into the festive hall. On the right hand stood all the little lady mice; and they whispered and giggled as if they were making fun of each other; on the left stood all the gentlemen mice, stroking their whiskers with their forepaws; and in the center of the hall the bridegroom and bride might be seen standing in a hollow cheese rind, and kissing each other terribly before all the guests.

More and more strangers kept flocking in. One mouse was nearly treading another to death; and the happy couple had stood themselves just in the little doorway, so that one could neither come in nor go out. Like the passage, the room had been greased with bacon rinds, and that was the entire dinner; but for the dessert a pea was brought out, in which a mouse belonging to the family had bitten the name of the happy couple—that is to say, the first letter of the name; that was something quite out of the common way.

All the mice said it was a beautiful wedding, and that the entertainment had been very jolly. And then Hjalmar drove home again; he had been in grand company, but he had been obliged to crawl through a mousehole, to make himself little, and to put on a tin soldier's uniform.

FRIDAY

"It is wonderful how many grown-up people there are who would be very glad to have me!" said Ole-Luk-Oie; "especially those who have done something wrong. 'Good little Ole,' they say to me, 'we cannot shut our eyes, and so we lie all night and see our bad deeds, which sit upon the bedstead like ugly little goblins, and throw hot water over us; will you not come and drive them away, so that we may have a good sleep?'—and then they sigh deeply—'We would really be glad to pay for it. Good night, Ole, the money lies on the windowsill.' But I do nothing for money," says Ole-Luk-Oie.

"What shall we do this evening?" asked Hjalmar.

"I don't know if you care to go to another wedding tonight. It is a different kind from that of yesterday. Your sister's great doll, that looks like a man, and is called Hermann, is going to marry the doll Bertha. Also, it is the doll's birthday, and so they will get very many presents."

"Yes, I know that," replied Hjalmar. "Whenever the dolls want new clothes, my sister lets them either keep their birthday or celebrate a wedding; that has certainly happened a hundred times already."

"Yes, but tonight is the hundred and first wedding; and when number one hundred and one is past, it is all over; and that is why it will be so splendid. Only look!"

And Hjalmar looked at the table. There stood the

little cardboard house with the windows lighted, and in front of it all the tin soldiers were presenting arms. The bride and bridegroom sat quite thoughtful, and with good reason, on the floor, leaning against a leg of the table. And Ole-Luk-Oie, dressed up in the grandmother's black gown, married them to each other. When the ceremony was over, all the pieces of furniture struck up the following beautiful song, which the pencil had written for them. It was sung to the melody of the soldiers' tattoo:

> "Let the song swell like the rushing wind,
> In honor of those who this day are joined,
> Although they stand here so stiff and blind,
> Because they are both of a leathery kind.
> Hurrah! hurrah! though they're deaf and blind,
> Let the song swell like the rushing wind."

And now they got their presents—but they had asked not to have any food given, for they intended to live on love.

"Shall we now go into a big summer lodging, or start on a journey?" asked the bridegroom.

And the swallow, who was a great traveler, and the old yard hen, who had brought up five broods of chickens, were consulted on the subject. And the swallow told of the beautiful warm countries, where the grapes hung in ripe, heavy clusters, where the air is mild, and the mountains glow with colors unknown here.

"But you have no red cabbage there!" said the

hen. "I was once in the country, with my children, in one summer that lasted five weeks. There was a sand pit, in which we could walk about and scratch, and we could go to a garden where red cabbage grew; it was so hot there that one could scarcely breathe. And then we have not all the poisonous animals that infest these warm countries of yours, and we are free from robbers. He who does not think our country the most beautiful—he certainly does not deserve to be here!" And then the hen cried, and went on, "I have also traveled. I rode in a coop about twelve miles, and there is no pleasure at all in traveling!"

"Yes, the hen is a sensible woman!" said the doll Bertha. "I don't think anything of traveling among mountains, for you only have to go up and then down again. No, we will go into the sand pit beyond the gate, and walk about the cabbage garden."

And so it was settled.

SATURDAY

"Am I to hear some stories now?" asked little Hjalmar, as soon as Ole-Luk-Oie had sent him to sleep.

"This evening we have no time for that," replied Ole-Luk-Oie; and he spread his finest umbrella over the lad. "Only look at these Chinamen!"

And the whole umbrella looked like a great China

dish, with blue trees and pointed bridges with little Chinamen upon them, who stood there nodding their heads.

"We must have the whole world prettily decorated for tomorrow morning," said Ole-Luk-Oie, "for that will be a holiday—it will be Sunday. I will go to the church steeples to see that the little church goblins are polishing the bells, that they may sound sweetly. I will go out into the field, and see if the breezes are blowing the dust from the grass and leaves; and, what is the greatest work of all, I will bring down all the stars, to polish them. I take them in my apron; but first each one must be numbered, and the holes in which they are to be placed up there must be numbered too; so that they may be placed in the same grooves again; or they would not sit fast, and we should have too many shooting stars, for one after another would fall down."

"Hark ye! Do you know, Mr. Ole-Luk-Oie," said an old portrait which hung upon the wall of the bedroom, where Hjalmar slept. "I am Hjalmar's great-grandfather! I thank you for telling the boy stories; but you must not mix up his ideas. The stars cannot come down and be polished! The stars are worlds, just like our own earth, and that is just the good thing about them."

"I thank you, old great-grandfather," said Ole-Luk-Oie, "I thank you! You are the head of the

family. But I am older than you! I am an old
heathen: the Romans and Greeks called me the
Dream God. I have been in the noblest houses, and
go there still! I know how to act with great people
and with small! Now you may tell your own
story!" And Ole-Luk-Oie took his umbrella and
went away.

"Well, well! May one not even give an opinion
nowadays?" grumbled the old portrait. And Hjalmar awoke.

SUNDAY

"Good evening!" said Ole-Luk-Oie; and Hjalmar
nodded, and then ran and turned his great-
grandfather's portrait against the wall, that it might
not interrupt them, as it had done yesterday.

"Now you must tell me stories—about the five
green peas that lived in one shell, and about the cock's
foot that paid court to the hen's foot, and of the
darning needle who gave herself such airs because she
thought herself a working needle."

"There may be too much of a good thing!" said
Ole-Luk-Oie. "You know that I would rather show
you something. I will show you my own brother.
His name, like mine, is Ole-Luk-Oie, but he never
comes to anyone more than once; and he takes him
to whom he comes upon his horse, and tells him
stories. He only knows two. One of these is so
beautiful that no one in the world can imagine it, and

the other is so horrible and dreadful that it cannot be described.

And then Ole-Luk-Oie lifted little Hjalmar up to the window, and said:

"There you will see my brother, the other Ole-Luk-Oie. They also call him Death! Do you see? He does not look so terrible as they make him in the picture books, where he is only a skeleton. No, that is silver embroidery that he has on his coat; that is a splendid uniform; a mantle of black velvet flies behind him over the horse. See how he gallops along!"

And Hjalmar saw how this Ole-Luk-Oie rode away, and took young people as well as old upon his his horse. Some of them he put before him, and some behind; but he always asked first—"How stands the mark-book?" "Good!" they all said. "Yes, but let me see it myself," he said. And then each one had to show him the book; and those who had "very well" and "remarkably well" written in their books, were placed in front of his horse, and a lovely story was told to them; while those who had "middling" or "fairly good," had to sit up behind, and hear a very terrible story indeed. They trembled and cried, and wanted to jump off the horse, but this they could not do, for they were all grown fast to it.

"But Death is a most splendid Ole-Luk-Oie," said Hjalmar. "I am not afraid of him!"

"Nor need you be," replied Ole-Luk-Oie; "but see that you have a good mark-book!"

"Yes, that is better!" muttered the great-grandfather's picture. "It is of some use giving one's opinion." And now he was satisfied.

You see, these are stories of Ole-Luk-Oie; and now he may tell you more himself, this evening!

The Marsh King's Daughter

ONCE a family of storks lived in the summertime on the roof of a Viking's house far up north.

One evening the Father Stork stayed out rather late, and when he came back he looked somewhat disturbed.

"I have something terrible to tell you!" he said to the Mother Stork.

"Don't tell it to me then," she answered; "remember that I am setting, it might upset me and that would be bad for the eggs!"

"You will have to know it," said he; "she has come here, the daughter of our king in Egypt. She has dared to take the journey, and now she has disappeared."

"The child of the fairies! Tell me all about it. You know I can't bear to be kept waiting now I am setting."

"Look here, Mother! She must have believed what the doctor said; she believed that the marsh

flowers up here would do something to help her
father get well, and she flew over here in feathers
with the other two princesses who have come north
every year to take the baths to make themselves
young. She came, and now she has gone."

"Your story is too long," said the Mother Stork,
"the eggs might get a chill, and I can't stand being
kept waiting."

"I have been watching," said the Father Stork,
"and tonight when I was among the reeds I saw three
swans flying along, and there was something that said
to me, 'Watch them, they are not real swans! They
are only in swan's feathers.'"

"Yes, indeed!" she said, "but tell me about the
Princess, I am quite tired of hearing about swan's
feathers."

"You know that in the middle of the bog there is
a kind of lake," said Father Stork. "You can see a
bit of it if you raise your head. Well there was a big
alder stump between the bushes and the quagmire,
and on this the three swans settled, flapping their
wings and looking about them. Then one of them
threw off the swan's feathers, and at once I knew that
she was the Princess from Egypt. There she sat with
no covering but her long black hair; I heard her beg
the two others to take good care of the swan's feathers
while she dived under the water to pick up the marsh
flower which she thought she could see. They
nodded and raised their heads, and lifted up the loose

feathers. What are they going to do with it, thought
I, and she no doubt asked them the same thing; and
the answer came: they flew up into the air with the
feathered cloak! 'Just you duck down,' they cried.
'Never again will you fly about like a swan; never
more will you see the land of Egypt; you may sit in
your swamp.' Then they tore the feather cloak into
a hundred bits, scattering feathers all over the place,
like a snowstorm; then away flew those two wicked
princesses."

"What a terrible thing," said Mother Stork; "but
I must hear the end of it."

"The Princess moaned and cried! Her tears
trickled down upon the alder stump, and then it began to move, for it was the Marsh King himself, who
lives in the bog. I saw the stump turn round, and
saw that it was no longer a stump; it stretched out
long branches like arms. The poor child was frightened, and she sprang away onto the shaking quagmire where it would not even bear my weight, far
less hers. She sank at once and the alder stump after
her, it was dragging her down. Great black bubbles
rose, and then there was nothing more to be seen.
Now she is buried in the Wild Bog and never will
she take back to Egypt the flowers for which she
came. You could not have endured the sight,
Mother!"

"You shouldn't even tell me anything of the sort
just now, it might have a bad effect upon the eggs.

The Princess must look after herself! She will get help somehow."

"I mean to keep a watch every day," said the stork, and he kept his word.

But a long time passed, and then one day he saw that a green stem shot up, and when it reached the top of the water, a leaf appeared at the top which grew broader and broader. Next a bud appeared close by it, and one morning at dawn, just as the stork was passing, the bud opened out in the warm rays of the sun, and in the middle of it lay a lovely baby, a little girl, looking just as fresh as if she had come out of a bath. She was so exactly like the Princess from Egypt that at first the stork thought it was she who had grown small; but when he put two and two together, he made up his mind, that it was her child and the Marsh King's. This explained why she lay in a water lily. "She can't stay there very long," thought the stork; "and there are too many of us in my nest as it is, but an idea has just come into my head! The Viking's Wife has no child, and she has often wished for one. As I am always said to bring the babies, this time I will do so. I will fly away to the Viking's Wife with the baby, and that will indeed be a joy for her."

So the stork took up the little girl and flew away with her to the timbered house where he picked a hole in the bladder skin which covered the window, and laid the baby in the arms of the Viking's Wife. This done, he flew home and told the Mother Stork all about it; and the young ones heard what he said. They were old enough to understand it.

"So you see that the Princess is not dead; she must have sent the baby up here and I have found a home for her."

"I said so from the very first," said the Mother Stork; "now just give a little care to your own children, it is almost time to start on our own journey. I feel a tingling in my wings every now and then! The cuckoo and the nightingale are already gone, and I hear from the quails that we shall soon have a good wind. Our young people will do themselves credit if I know them aright!"

How delighted the Viking's Wife was when she woke in the morning and found the little baby on her bosom. She kissed and hugged it; but it screamed and kicked terribly, and seemed anything but happy. At last it cried itself to sleep, and as it lay there a prettier little thing could not have been seen. The Viking's Wife was delighted. She was sure that now her husband and all his men would soon come back suddenly. So she and her household busied themselves in putting the house in order. The Viking's Wife helped with all this work herself, so that when evening came she was very tired and slept soundly. When she woke towards morning she was much frightened at finding that the little baby had gone. She sprang up and lighted a pine chip and looked about. There was no baby, but at the foot of the bed sat a hideous toad. She was horrified and seized up a heavy stick to kill it, but it looked at her with such sad eyes that she had not the heart to strike it. Once more she looked round and the toad gave a faint pitiful croak which made her start. She ran across the room and threw open the window shutter; the sun was just rising, and its beams fell upon the bed and the great toad. All at once the monster's wide mouth seemed to grow small, and to become small and rosy, the limbs stretched and again took their lovely shapes, and it was her own dear little baby which lay there, and not a hideous frog.

"Whatever is this?" she cried; "I have had a bad dream. This is my own darling child." She kissed it and pressed it to her heart, but it struggled and bit like a wild kitten.

Neither that day nor the next did the Viking lord come home, although he was on his way, but the winds were against him; they were blowing southward for the storks.

In the course of a few days and nights the Viking's Wife saw that some magic power had a terrible hold over her baby. In the daytime it was as beautiful as any fairy, but it had a bad wicked temper; at night, on the other hand, she became a hideous toad, quiet and still, with sad mournful eyes. The reason was that the little girl by day had her mother's form and her father's evil temper; but at night she had her father's form, and her mother's sweet nature and gentle spirit beamed out of the monster. Who could free her from the power of this witchcraft? It caused the Viking's Wife much grief and trouble, and yet her heart loved the unhappy child. She knew that she would never dare to tell her husband the truth, because he would have the poor child laid on the highway for anyone who chose to look after it. The good woman had not the heart to do this, and so she decided that he should only see the child by broad daylight.

One morning there was a sound of stork's wings swishing over the roof; during the night more than a hundred pairs of storks had made it their resting place, and they were now trying their wings before starting on their long southward flight.

"Every man ready!" cried the leader, looking over his flock; "all the wives and children, too."

"How light we feel," cried the young storks; "our legs tingle as if we were full of live frogs! How splendid it is to be traveling to foreign lands."

"Keep in line!" said the father and mother, "and don't let your beaks clatter so fast, it isn't good for the chest." Then away they flew.

At the very same moment a horn sounded over the

hill. The Viking had landed with all his men; they were bringing home no end of rich treasures.

What life and noise came to the Viking's home! The Viking's Wife sat on the cross bench in the great hall. She was dressed in silk with gold bracelets and large amber beads. The minstrel brought her name into his song; he spoke of the golden treasure she had brought to her husband, and his delight at the beautiful child.

The Viking went out once more that year on a raid, although the fall winds were beginning; he sailed with his men to the coast of Britain. His wife stayed at home with the little girl, and she soon grew fonder of the poor toad with the sad eyes than she was of the little beauty who tore and bit.

The storks were in the land of Egypt under such a sun as we have on a warm summer's day! The Nile waters had gone down and the land was full of frogs; to the stork this was the most splendid sight. The eyes of the young ones were quite dazzled with the sight.

"See what it is to be here, and we always have the same in our warm country," said the mother stork, and the stomachs of the little ones tingled.

The old ones stayed in their nests on the slender temple towers resting themselves, but at the same time busily smoothing their feathers and rubbing their beaks upon their red stockings. Or they would lift up their long necks and gravely bow their heads. The young storks walked gravely among the juicy reeds; they would swallow a frog at every third step, or walk about with a small snake dangling from their beak, it looked so pretty. There was sunshine every day, and plenty to eat; nothing to think of but pleasure!

But in the great palace of their Egyptian king matters were not so pleasant. The rich and mighty lord lay stretched upon his couch, as stiff in every limb as if he had been a mummy. The great painted hall was as gorgeous as if he had been lying within a tulip. Friends stood around him—he was not dead—yet he could hardly be called living. The healing marsh flower from the northern lands, which was to be found and plucked by one who loved him best, would never be brought. His young and lovely daughter, who in the feathers of a swan had flown over the sea and land to the far north, would never come back. The two wicked swan princesses had come back and this is the story they told.

"We were flying high up in the air when a hunter saw us and shot his arrow; it pierced our young friend to the heart and she slowly sank. As she sank she sang her farewell song and fell into the midst of a forest pool. There by the shore under a drooping birch we buried her. Never more will she come back to Egypt."

Then they both cried. But the Father Stork who

heard it clattered with his beak and said, "Pack of lies; I should like to drive my beak right into their breasts!"

"I think I will snatch away the swans' feathers from the two wicked princesses," said the Father Stork. "Then they could not go to the Wild Bog to do any more mischief. I will keep the feathers up there till we find a use for them."

"Up where will you keep them?" asked the Mother Stork.

"In our nest at the Wild Bog," said he. "The young ones and I can carry them between us, and if they are too heavy, there are places enough on the way where we can hide them till our next flight. One wing would be enough for her, but two are better; it is a good plan to have plenty of wraps in a northern country!"

"You will get no thanks for it," said the Mother Stork, "but you are the master. I have nothing to say except when I am setting."

In the meantime the little child in the Viking's hall by the Wild Bog, whither the storks flew in the spring, had had a name given her: it was Helga, but such a name was far too gentle for such a wild spirit as lived in her. Month by month it showed itself more, and year by year while the storks took the same journey,

She rode a horse bareback as if she were part of it, nor did she jump off while he bit and fought with the other wild horses.

in the fall towards the Nile, and in spring towards the Wild Bog. The little child grew to be a big girl, and before one knew how, she was the loveliest maiden of sixteen. She rode a horse bareback as if she were a part of it, nor did she jump off while he bit and fought with the other wild horses. She would often throw herself from the cliff into the sea in all her clothes, and swim out to meet the Viking when his boat neared the shore; and she cut off the longest strand of her beautiful long hair to string her bow.

The Viking's Wife was now an anxious mother, because she knew that a spell rested over the terrible child. Often when her mother stepped out on the balcony Helga, from pure love of teasing it seemed, would sit upon the edge of the well, throw up her hands and feet, and go backwards plump into the dark narrow hole. Here with her frog's nature she would rise again and clamber out like a cat dripping with water, carrying a perfect stream into the banqueting hall, washing aside the green twigs strewn on the floor.

One thing, however, always held little Helga in check, and that was twilight; when it drew near she became quiet, allowing herself to be called and guided. Then she drew close to her mother, and when the sun sank she sat sad and quiet, shrivelled up into the form of a toad. Her body was now much bigger than those creatures ever are, but for that reason all the more ugly. There was something piteous in her eyes;

and voice she had none, only a hollow croak like the smothered sobs of a dreaming child. Then the Viking's Wife would take it on her knee, and looking into its eyes would forget the ugly form, and would often say, "I could almost wish that thou wouldst always be my dumb frog child. Thou art more terrible to look at when thou art clothed in beauty." Then she would write charms against her sickness and wickedness, and throw them over the miserable girl, but they did no good at all.

The Viking came home early that fall with his treasures and prisoners; among these was a young Christian priest. The young priest was put in prison in the deep stone cellars of the timber house and his feet and hands were bound with strips of bark.

The ugly toad crouched in the corner that night, and all was still. She took a step forward and listened, then she stepped forward again and grasped the heavy bar of the door with her clumsy hands. Softly she drew it back, and lifted the latch, then took up the lamp which stood in the anteroom. It seemed as if a strong power gave her strength. She drew out the iron bolt from the barred cellar door, and slipped in to the prisoner. He was asleep, she touched him with her cold clammy hand, and when he awoke and saw the hideous creature, he shuddered. She drew out her knife and cut his bonds apart, and then beckoned him to follow her. He asked, "Who art thou?"

The toad only beckoned him and led him behind the sheltering curtains down a long passage to the stable, pointed to a horse, on to which he sprang and she after him. She sat in front of him clutching the mane of the animal. The prisoner understood her, and they rode at a quick pace along a path he never would have found to the heath. He forgot her hideous form, knowing that the mercy of the Lord worked through the spirits of darkness. He prayed and sang holy songs which made her tremble. Was it the power of prayer and his singing working upon her, or was it the chill air of the coming dawn? What were her feelings? She raised herself and wanted to stop and jump off the horse, but the Christian priest held her tightly, with all his strength, and sang aloud a psalm as if this could lift the spell which held her.

The horse bounded on more wildly than before, the sky grew red, and the first sunbeams pierced the clouds. As the stream of light touched her, she was once more a lovely girl, but her evil spirit was the same. The priest held a blooming girl in his arms and he was terrified at the sight. He stopped the horse and sprang down. But young Helga sprang to the ground too. She tore the sharp knife from her belt and rushed upon the startled man. "Let me get at thee," she cried, "let me reach thee and my knife shall pierce thee!"

She closed upon him and they wrestled together,

but an unseen power seemed to give strength to the Christian; he held her tight, and the old oak under which they stood seemed to help him, for the loosened roots above the ground tripped her up. Close by rose a bubbling spring and he sprinkled her with water and commanded the evil spirit to leave her, making the sign of the cross over her. Her arms fell, and she looked with paling cheeks at this man who seemed to be a mighty magician skilled in secret arts. She trembled now as he traced the sign of the cross upon her forehead and bosom, and sat before him with drooping head like a wild bird tamed.

He spoke gently to her about the deed of love she had done for him this night, when she came in the hideous shape of a toad, cut his bonds, and led him out to light and life. She herself was bound, he said, and with stronger ties than his; but she also, through him, should reach to light and life.

She allowed herself to be lifted on to the horse's back, and sat there like one in a dream.

The Christian man bound together two branches in the shape of a cross, which he held aloft in his hand as he rode through the wood. They rode out of the wood, over a hill, and again through trackless forests. Towards evening they met a band of robbers.

"Where hast thou stolen this beautiful child?" they

cried, stopping the horse and pulling down the two riders, for they were many.

The priest had no weapon but the knife which he had taken from little Helga, and with this he struck out right and left. One of the robbers raised his ax, but the Christian sprang on one side, or he would certainly have been hit; but the blade flew into the horse's neck, so that the blood gushed forth, and it fell to the ground dead. Then little Helga, as if roused from a long dream, rushed forward and threw herself on to the gasping horse. The priest placed himself in front of her as a shield and defense; but one of the robbers swung his iron club at his head, and he fell upon the ground.

The robbers seized little Helga by her white arms, but the sun was just going down, and as the last rays vanished she was changed into the form of a frog. A greenish-white mouth stretched half over her face; her arms became thin and slimy; while broad hands, with webbed fingers, spread themselves out like fans. The robbers in fear let her go, and she stood among them a hideous monster; and bounded away with great leaps as high as herself, and disappeared in the thicket. Then the robbers knew that this must be some evil spirit, and they hurried away.

The full moon had arisen and was shining in all its splendor when little Helga, in the form of a frog, crept out of the thicket. She stopped by the body of the Christian priest and the dead horse; she looked at them with pity; a sob came from the toad like that of a child bursting into tears. She threw herself down, first upon one, and then on the other; and brought water in her hand, which, from being large and webbed, formed a cup. This she sprinkled them with; but they did not awake. She dug into the ground as deep as she could; she wished to dig a grave for them. She had nothing but the branch of a tree and her two hands, and she tore the web between her fingers till the blood ran from them. She brought large boughs to cover him, and scattered dried leaves between the branches. Then she brought the heaviest stones she could carry, and laid them over the body, filling up the spaces with moss. Now the sun was rising, and there stood little Helga in all her beauty with bleeding hands and tears for the first time on her cheeks.

The cross made of branches, the last work of the Christian, still lay by the grave. Little Helga took it up, and placed it between the stones which covered man and horse. At the sad memory her tears burst forth again, and she traced a cross in the earth round the grave—and as she formed with both hands the holy sign, the webbed skin fell away from her fingers like a torn glove. She washed her hands at the spring and looked in wonder at their delicate whiteness.

The frog's skin fell away from her, she was the

beautiful young girl, but her head bent wearily and her limbs needed rest. She slept. But her sleep was short, she was awakened at midnight; before her stood the horse prancing and full of life, which shone forth from his eyes and his wounded neck. Close by his side she saw the Christian priest, surrounded by flames of fire.

Then he lifted Helga on the horse and together they rode, singing, southward. They came to a beautiful stream. The water lilies spread themselves over the surface of the pool like a carpet of wrought flowers, and on this carpet lay a sleeping woman. She was young and beautiful; little Helga fancied she saw herself, her picture mirrored in the quiet pool. It was her mother she saw, the wife of the Marsh King, the Princess from the river Nile.

The priest lifted the sleeping woman up on to the horse, and all three rode on through the air to dry ground. Just then the cock crew from the Viking's hall, and the dream melted away, but mother and daughter stood side by side.

"Is it myself I see reflected in the deep water?" said the mother.

"Do I see myself mirrored in a bright shield?" said the daughter. But as they clasped each other heart to heart, the mother's heart beat the fastest, and she understood.

"My child, my own heart's blossom, my lotus out

of the deep waters!" and she wept over her daughter.

While they stood there pressed heart to heart the stork was wheeling above their heads in great circles; at length he flew away to his nest and brought back the swan feathers so long cherished there. He threw one over each of them; the feathers closed over them closely, and mother and daughter rose into the air as two white swans.

"And the lotus flower which I was to take with me," said the Egyptian Princess, "flies by my side in a swan's feathers. I take the flower of my heart with me. Now for home! home!"

But Helga said she could not leave the Danish land without seeing her loving foster-mother once more, the Viking's Wife. For in Helga's memory now rose up every tender word and every tear her foster-mother had shed over her, and it almost seemed as if she loved this mother best.

"Yes, we must go to the Viking's hall," said the Father Stork; "Mother and the young ones are waiting for us there. How they will open their eyes and flap their wings! Mother doesn't say much; she is somewhat short, but she means very well. Now I will make a great clattering to let them know we are coming!"

So he clattered with his beak, and he and the swans flew off to the Viking's hall.

They all lay in a deep sleep within; the Viking's Wife had gone late to rest, for she was in great anxiety about little Helga, who had not been seen for three days.

Suddenly before her stood little Helga in all the radiance of her beauty, gentle as she had never been before, and with gleaming eyes. She kissed her foster-mother's hands, and thanked her for all the care and love she had shown in the days of her trial and misery. Little Helga rose up as a great white swan and spread her wings, with the rushing sound of a flock of birds of passage on the wing.

The Viking's Wife was awakened by the rushing sound of wings outside; she knew it was the time when the storks took their flight, and it was these she heard. She wanted to see them once more and to bid them good-by, so she got up and went out on the balcony; she saw stork upon stork sitting on the roofs of the outbuildings round the courtyard, and flocks of them were flying round and round in great circles. Just in front of her, on the edge of the well where little Helga so often had frightened her with her wildness, sat two white swans, who looked at her with their wise eyes.

"Are those the high mountains I used to hear about?" asked Helga in the swan's feathers.

"Those are thunder clouds driving along beneath us," said her mother.

"What are those white clouds that rise so high?" again inquired Helga.

"Those are mountains covered with snow that you

see yonder," said her mother, as they flew across the Alps down towards the blue Mediterranean.

"Africa's land! Egypt's strand!" sang the daughter of the Nile in her joy, as from far above, in her swan's feathers, her eye fell upon the narrow waving yellow line, her birthplace.

"The storks have come back," was said in the great house on the Nile, where its lord lay in the great hall on his downy cushions covered with a leopard skin, scarcely alive, and yet not dead either, waiting and hoping for the lotus flower from the deep marsh in the north.

Friends and servants stood around his couch, when two great white swans who had come with the storks flew into the hall. They threw off their dazzling wings, and there stood two beautiful women as like each other as twin drops of dew. They bent over the pale withered old man, throwing back their long hair.

As little Helga bent over her grandfather, the color came back to his cheeks and new life came to his limbs. The old man rose with new health and energy; his daughter and granddaughter clasped him in their arms, as if with a joyous morning greeting after a long troubled night.

Joy reigned throughout the house and in the stork's nest too, but there the rejoicing was chiefly over the plentiful food, especially the swarms of frogs.

"Surely you will be made something at last," whispered the Mother Stork.

"Oh, what should I be made?" said the Father Stork, "and what have I done? Nothing at all!"

"You have done more than all the others! Without you and the young ones the two Princesses would never have seen Egypt again, nor would the old man have got back his health."

Early in the spring, when the storks were again about to take flight to the north, little Helga took off her gold bracelet, and, scratching her name on it, beckoned to Father Stork and put it round his neck. She told him to take it to the Viking's Wife, who would see by it that her foster-daughter still lived, was happy, and had not forgotten her.

"It is a heavy thing to carry!" thought Father Stork, as it slipped on to his neck; "but neither gold nor honor are to be thrown upon the highway! The stork brings good luck, they say up there!"

"You lay gold, and I lay eggs," said Mother Stork; "but you only lay once and I lay every year. But no one appreciates us!"

"One always knows when one has done well, though, Mother!" said Father Stork.

"But you can't hang it outside," said Mother Stork; "it never gives a full meal!"

In the fall an eagle perched on one of the Pyramids saw a gorgeous train of heavily laden camels and men

clad in armor riding fiery Arab horses as white as silver
with red nostrils and flowing manes reaching to the
ground. A royal prince from Arabia, as handsome
as a prince should be, was coming to the stately palace
where now the storks' nest stood empty; the storks
were still in their northern home; but they would soon
now come—nay, on the very day when the rejoicings
were at their height they came. They were happy
days, and little Helga was the bride clad in rich silk
and many jewels. The bridegroom was the young
prince from Arabia, and they sat together at the upper
end of the table between the mother and her grandfather.

Just then there was a rustle of great wings in the
air outside; the storks had come back. And the old
couple, tired as they were and needing rest, flew
straight down to the railing of the veranda; they knew
nothing about the festivities. They had heard on the
frontiers of the country that little Helga had them
painted on the wall, for they belonged to the story of
her life.

"It was prettily done of her," said Father Stork.

"It is little enough," said Mother Stork; "they could
hardly do less."

Hans Clodhopper ↻

FAR away in the country lay an old house where lived an old squire who had two sons. They thought themselves so clever that, if they had known only half of what they thought they knew, it would have been enough. They both wanted to marry the king's daughter, for she had said that she would have for her husband the man who knew best how to choose his words.

Both took a whole week to get ready, which was the longest time allowed them; but, after all, it was quite long enough, for they both had lots of book learning, and everyone knows how useful that is. One knew the whole Latin dictionary and three years' issue of the daily paper of the town off by heart, so that he could recite it all backward or forward, as you pleased. The other had worked at the city laws and knew by heart what every alderman ought to know, so that he thought he could speak on state matters quite well and give his opinion. He understood, besides this, how to embroider with roses and other flowers, for he was very ready with his fingers.

"I shall win the king's daughter!" they both said at once.

Their old father gave each of them a fine horse; the one who knew the dictionary and the daily paper by heart had a black horse, while the other who was so clever at law had a milk-white one. Then they oiled the corners of their mouths so that they might be able to speak more fluently. All the servants stood in the courtyard and saw them mount, and here by chance came the third brother; for the squire had three sons, but nobody counted him with his brothers, for he was not so learned as they were and he was generally called Hans Clodhopper.

"Oh! oh!" said Hans. "Where are you off to? You are in your Sunday best clothes!"

"We are going to the court to woo the Princess! Don't you know what everybody knows throughout all the country?" And they told him about it.

"Hurrah! I'll go too!" cried Hans Clodhopper; and the brothers laughed at him and rode off.

"Dear father!" cried Hans, "I must have a horse. I must get married too. If she will have me she will have me, and if she won't have me I will have her."

"Stop that nonsense!" said the old man. "I will not give you a horse. You can't speak; you don't know how to choose your words. Your brothers! Ah, they are very fine fellows!"

"Well," said Hans, "if I can't have a horse I will take a goat which is mine. He can carry me!"

And he did so. He sat astride on the goat, struck his heels into its side, and went rattling down the high-road like a hurricane.

Hoppetty-hop! what a ride! "Here I come!" shouted Hans, singing so that the echoes were roused far and near. But his brothers were riding slowly in front. They were not speaking, but they were think-ing over all the good things they were going to say, for everything had to be thought out.

"Hullo!" bawled Hans; "here I am! Just look what I found on the road!" And he showed them a dead crow which he had picked up.

"Clodhopper!" said his brothers, "what are you going to do with it?"

"With the crow? I shall give it to the Princess!"

"Do so, certainly!" they said, laughing loudly and riding on.

"Slap! bang! here I am again! Look what I have just found! You don't find such things every day on the road!"

And the brothers looked around to see what in the world he could have found.

"Clodhopper!" said they, "that is an old wooden shoe without the top! Are you going to send that, too, to the princess?"

"Of course I shall!" answered Hans; and the brothers laughed and rode on a good way.

"Slap! bang! here I am!" cried Hans; "better and better—it is really famous!"

"What have you found now?" asked the brothers.

"Oh," said Hans, "it is really too good! How pleased the Princess will be!"

"Why!" said the brothers, "this is mud, straight from the ditch."

"Of course it is!" said Hans, "and it is the best kind! Look how it runs through one's fingers!" And so saying he filled his pockets with the mud.

But the brothers rode on so fast that dust and sparks flew all around, and they reached the gate of the town a good hour before Hans. Here came the suitors. Each had a ticket and a number, and they were ranged in rows, six in each row, and they were so tightly packed that they could not move their arms. This was a very good thing, for otherwise they would have torn each other in pieces, just because the one was in front of the other.

All the country people were standing round the king's throne, and were crowded together in thick masses almost out of the windows to see the Princess receive the suitors; and as each one came into the room all his fine words went out like a candle!

"No good!" said the Princess. "Away! out with him!"

At last she came to the row in which the brother who knew the dictionary by heart was, but he did not know it any longer; he had quite forgotten it while standing in the rank and file. And the floor creaked and the ceiling was all made of glass mirrors, so that he saw himself standing on his head, and by each window were standing three reporters and an editor; and each of them was writing down what was said, to publish it in the paper that came out and was sold at the street corners for a penny. It was fearful, and they had made up the fire so that it was red-hot.

"It is hot in here, isn't it?" said the suitor, wiping his forehead.

"Of course it is! My father is roasting young chickens today!" said the Princess.

"Ahem!" There he stood like an idiot. He was not ready for such a speech; he did not know what to say, although he wanted to say something witty. "Ahem!"

"No good!" said the Princess. "Take him out!" and out he had to go.

Now the other brother entered.

"How hot is is!" he said.

"Of course! We are roasting young chickens to-day!" said the Princess."

"How do you—um!" he said, and the reporters wrote down, "How do you—um."

"No good!" said the Princess. "Take him out!"

"Oh, rather!" said Hans Clodhopper. *"Here is a cooking pot."*

Now Hans Clodhopper came in. He rode his goat right into the hall.

"I say! How roasting hot it is here!" said he.

"Of course! I am roasting young chickens today!" said the Princess.

"That's good!" replied Hans Clodhopper. "Then can I roast a crow with them?"

"With the greatest of pleasure!" said the Princess; "but have you anything you can roast it in? I have neither pot nor saucepan."

"Oh, rather!" said Hans Clodhopper. "Here is a cooking pot with tin rings," and he drew out the old wooden shoe and laid the crow in it.

"That is quite a meal!" said the Princess; "but where shall we get the soup from?"

"I've got that in my pocket!" said Hans Clodhopper. "I have so much that I can throw some away!" and he poured some mud out of his pocket.

"I like you!" said the Princess. "You can answer and you can speak, and I will marry you. But do you know that every word which we are saying and have said has been taken down and will be in the paper tomorrow? By each window, do you see, there are standing three reporters and an old editor, and this old editor is the worst, for he doesn't understand anything!" But she only said this to tease Hans. And the reporters giggled and each dropped a blot of ink on the floor.

"Ah! are those the great people?" said Hans. "Then I will give the editor the best!" So saying, he turned his pockets inside out and threw the mud right in his face.

"That was neatly done!" said the Princess. "I couldn't have done it, but I will soon try to learn."

So Hans became king, got a wife and a crown, and sat on the throne; and this we have still fresh from the newspaper of the editor and the reporters—and you cannot believe them for a moment.

The Garden of Paradise ✑

THERE was once a king's son who had all sorts of picture books, but none of them said anything about the Garden of Paradise, and that was just what he wanted to read about. One day when he was walking in the forest he came upon a great cave. He looked in, and saw a stag being roasted on a huge fire. An old woman, big and strong, who looked like a man, sat by the fire.

"Come in and get yourself dried," said the old woman, for the young Prince had been caught in the rain.

He entered the cave and sat down by the fire. "There is a nasty draft here," he said.

"It will be worse when my sons come home," said the woman. "You are in the Cave of the Winds, and my sons are the four winds of heaven. Here is one of them now."

It was the North Wind who came in with icy coldness.

Hailstones bounded about the floor, and snowflakes floated in the air. He was clad in a bear's skin with a sealskin cap, which came down over his ears; long icicles hung down from his beard.

"Do not go too suddenly to the fire," said the Prince. "If you do, your hands and feet will be frostbitten."

"Frost!" the North Wind said, and burst out laughing. "Why, it is just frost I love more than anything else. I come from the Polar Sea where there is nothing but frost. But here comes West Wind."

The West Wind looked like a wild man. His hair was all shaggy and he carried a great mahogany club from one of the far western forests.

Now came the South Wind, wearing a turban and a long flowing gown like a Bedouin of the desert. "It is terribly cold here," he said, coming close to the fire.

"Nonsense!" said the North Wind. "It is so hot I can hardly breathe!"

Then in came the East Wind, dressed like a Chinese.

"Oh, do you come from the Garden of Paradise?" asked the Prince.

"No. But I go there tomorrow," said the East Wind.

"Please, oh please, take me there!" pleaded the Prince.

So the next day, after the Prince had had a good night's sleep, the East Wind carried him away to the

Garden of Paradise. It was full of palm trees and lovely flowers and singing birds. "Oh, this is wonderful!" cried the Prince. Then he found that a beautiful Fairy was standing beside him.

"So you like our Garden?" she said.

"Indeed I do," said the Prince. "I would like to live here all my life."

"That cannot be," said the Fairy. "At least, not for ever so many years. The East Wind likes to bring little boys here now and then, just to show them what a beautiful place the Garden of Paradise is. But he must whisk them back to their homes right away."

"And you are going to send me away too?" asked the Prince with tears in his eyes.

"Indeed I am," said the Fairy. "But if you are good all through your life, the East Wind will bring you to the Garden, and you can stay here forever and ever."

So saying she disappeared, and the East Wind suddenly sprang upon the Prince and carried him off. He fell asleep, and when he awoke he was back in his home. But he was happy now, for he knew all about the Garden of Paradise. Strange to say, he never again saw the Cave of the Winds.

The Tinderbox ∿

A SOLDIER came marching along the highroad—one, two! one, two! He had his knapsack at his back and his sword at his side, for he had been in the wars, and was now going home.

He fell in with an old witch on the road—oh, she was so frightful! for her under lip hung down right upon her breast. "Good-day, soldier," she said; "what a beautiful sword and large knapsack you have! You are a real soldier, and you shall have as much money as you can possibly wish for."

"Thank you, old witch!" the soldier said.

"Do you see that large tree there?" the witch said, pointing to one which stood by the side of the road. "It is quite hollow, and if you climb to the top you will see a hole, through which you can let yourself down, right to the bottom of it. I will tie a rope round your body, so as to pull you up when you call to me."

"And what am I to do down there, inside the tree?" the soldier asked.

"Bring money," the witch said. "For you must know, that when you reach the bottom of the tree, you will find yourself in a large hall, lighted by more than a hundred lamps. Then you will see three doors, which you can open, for the keys are in the locks. If you go into the first room you will see, in the middle of the floor, a large box on which a dog is seated; it has eyes like big teacups, but you need not mind it. I will give you my blue check apron, which you must spread out upon the floor, then walk straight up to the dog, lay hold of it and place it upon my apron; then you can take out as many pennies as you like. It is all copper money; but if you would rather have silver you must go into the next room. There sits a dog with eyes as large as the wheels of a water-mill, but do not let that trouble you, for if you place it on my apron you can take the money. If, however, you prefer gold, you can have that too, and as much of it as you like to carry, by going into the third room. But the dog seated on the money-box has two eyes, each one as big as the Round Tower of Copenhagen. That is a dog! but never mind him, only put him upon my apron, then he will not hurt you, and you can take as much gold out of the box as you like."

There sat the dog with eyes like big cups, staring at him.

"That is not so bad," the soldier said; "but what must I give you, you old witch, for, of course, you want something?"

"No," the witch said, "not a single penny do I want. For me you need only bring an old tinderbox, which my grandmother forgot the last time she was in there."

"Well, then, tie the rope round me at once," the soldier said.

"Here it is," the witch said; "and here, too, is my blue check apron."

Then the soldier climbed up the tree, let himself slip down through the hole, and found himself, as the witch had said, down below, in the large hall where the many hundred lamps were burning.

Now he opened the first door, and, sure enough, there sat the dog with eyes like big cups, staring at him.

"Well, you are a pretty fellow," the soldier said, placed him upon the apron, and filled his pockets with pennies, after which he locked the box, and having put the dog back upon it, went into the next room, where he found the dog with eyes like mill wheels.

"Now, you shouldn't look at me in that way, for it may strain your eyes and hurt your sight," the soldier said. He then seated the dog upon the apron; and no sooner did he see all the silver in the box than he threw away the copper money he had, and filled his pockets and knapsack with the silver. He then

went into the third room, and it was an ugly beast he
saw there. The dog's eyes were, indeed, as large as
the Round Tower, and kept turning around in its head
exactly like mill wheels.

"Good-day to you," the soldier said, touching his
cap, for such a dog he had never seen in all his life,
but after looking at him for a time, he thought that
was enough, so he took him down and opened the
box. Good gracious! what a quantity of gold was
there! With that he could buy the whole of Copenhagen, and all the gingerbread horses, all the tin soldiers, whips, and rocking-horses in the whole world.
There was a lot of gold! He now threw out all the
silver with which he had filled his pockets and knapsack, and put in the gold instead. Yes, his pockets,
the knapsack, his cap, and even his boots, were filled
with it, so that he could scarcely walk. He was now
rich, so he put the dog back on the box, shut the
door, and called out to the old witch—

"Now pull me up."

"And have you got the tinderbox?" the old witch
asked.

"Well, to be sure, I had forgotten that," the soldier
said, so he went back and fetched it. The witch pulled
him up, and there he stood again on the highroad,
but with his pockets, his knapsack, cap, and boots
filled with gold.

"And what do you intend to do with the tinder-box?" he asked.

"That is no business of yours," the witch said. "You have got your gold, so give me my tinderbox."

"What does this mean?" the soldier cried; "tell me at once what you want to do with the tinderbox, or I'll draw my sword and cut off your head."

"No," the wicked witch said.

So the soldier cut off her head, and there she lay. But he tied up all his gold in her apron, slung it across his shoulder, and, thrusting the tinderbox into his pocket, walked on, straight to the town.

That was a beautiful town, and he turned into the very grandest hotel, where he reserved the best rooms, and ordered his favorite dishes, for he was rich now that he had so much money.

The servant, as he cleaned his boots, thought that they were most wretched things to belong to so rich a gentleman, for he had not yet bought any new ones, but the next day he got good boots and fine clothes. Now the soldier had become a gentleman, and he was told of all the wonders that were to be seen in the town, of the King, and what a pretty princess his daughter was.

"How can one get to see her?" the soldier asked.

"She is not to be seen at all," they all said, "for she lives in a brass castle surrounded by many walls and towers. No one but the King himself can go in and out there, for it has been prophesied that she will be married to a common soldier, and the King cannot consent to that."

"I should like to see her," the soldier thought, but nohow could he gain permission to do so.

Now he led a merry life, visited the theater, drove about in the King's garden, and gave a great deal of money to the poor, which was very good of him; but he remembered from when he was poor, how wretched it is not to have a penny. He was now rich, had beautiful clothes and many friends, who all said that he was a first-rate fellow and a real gentleman, which the soldier liked to hear. But as he spent money every day and never got any, it happened after a while that he only had a shilling left; so he had to give up his splendid rooms, where he had lived, and go into a small garret under the tiles, and clean and mend his own boots; and no more of his friends came to see him, for there were so many stairs to mount.

It had grown quite dark and he could not even buy a candle, but then he remembered that there was a small one in the tinderbox which he had got out of the hollow tree. He got the flint and steel out of the box, and no sooner had he struck a few sparks, than the dog, which had eyes as big as a teacup and which he had seen in the tree, stood before him, and said, "What are your commands, sir?"

"How is this?" he said. "That is a good sort of tinderbox, if I can so easily get all I want by means of it. Get me some money," he said to the dog. In an instant it was gone, and almost at the same moment was back again, with a purse of money in its jaws.

Now the soldier knew what a fine tinderbox it was. If he struck the flint once the dog that sat on the box containing the copper money appeared; if twice, that which had care of the silver; and if three times, there came the dog that guarded the gold. The soldier now moved back to his splendid rooms, and bought some more fine clothes, when at once all his friends knew him again and made much of him.

It seemed to him one day that it was something very strange there was no seeing the Princess. Every-one said that she was very beautiful, but what was the good of that if she was always to be shut up in the brazen castle with the many towers? "Cannot I get to see her anyhow?" he said; "where is my tinder-box?" He struck fire, and at once the dog with eyes like a teacup appeared.

"It is true it is the middle of the night," the soldier said, "but I should so very much like to see the Prin-cess, only for a moment."

The dog was gone in a moment, and before the soldier thought it possible was back again with the Princess. She was lying asleep on its back, and so lovely, that everyone could see at once she was a real princess. The soldier could not possibly resist kissing her, for he was a true soldier.

Then the dog ran back with the Princess, but the next morning when the King and Queen were taking their breakfast with her she said she had had the strangest dream of a dog and a soldier. That she had ridden on the dog, and the soldier had kissed her.

"That is a pretty story indeed!" the Queen said.

It was now settled that the next night one of the old ladies of the court should sit up by the Princess's bedside, in order to see whether it was really a dream, or how it might be.

The soldier had a strong wish to see the Princess again, so the dog came in the night, took her up, and ran off as fast as possible, but the old lady at once put on a pair of magic boots and followed quite as quickly. When she saw that they went into a large house, she thought, "Now I'll know where it is," so she made a large cross on the door with a piece of chalk. She then went home to bed, and the dog came back with the Princess. But the dog had seen that a cross was chalked on the door of the house where the soldier lived, so he took a piece of chalk too, and made a cross on all the doors of the town, which was cleverly done, for now the old lady could not find the proper door, as there were crosses on them all.

Early the next morning the King and Queen, the

The dog was gone in a moment, and before the soldier thought it possible, was back again with the Princess.

old lady, and all the officers of the court came to see where the Princess had been.

"Here it is," the King said, when he saw the first door with the cross upon it.

"No, there it is, my dear husband," the Queen said, seeing the second door with the cross.

"But here is one, and there is one," they all said, for whichever way they looked, there was a cross on the door, so they saw well that their looking would be of no use.

The Queen, however, was a very clever woman, and could do more things than drive in her carriage, so she took her large golden scissors, cut up a large piece of silk, and made a pretty little bag, which she filled with buckwheat meal and tied it round the Princess's neck. When this was done, she cut a small hole in the bag, so that the meal falling out would strew the road the whole way the Princess might take.

In the night the dog came again, took the Princess on his back, and carried her to the soldier, who loved her dearly, and wished so much he were a prince that he might marry her.

The dog did not notice how the meal strewed the whole of the way, from the castle to the soldier's window, where he ran up the wall with the Princess. The following morning the King and Queen saw plainly where their daughter had been, so they had the soldier taken and put in prison.

There he was, and oh! how dark and frightful it

was there, nor was it cheering when he was told,
"Tomorrow you are to be hanged." It was not
pleasant to hear, and his tinderbox he had left behind
him at the hotel. In the morning he could see, through
the bars of his prison window, how the people were
hurrying to the place of execution to see him hanged.
He heard the drum, and saw the soldiers marching.
All were running to get out of the town in time, and
among the rest a shoemaker's boy with his apron on,
and in slippers, one of which flew off as he ran along,
right against the wall, where the soldier was looking
out through the prison window.

"Here, you shoemaker's boy," the soldier said to
him, "you need not hurry so, for there will be nothing
to see till I come; but if you will run to where I lived
and fetch me my tinderbox, you shall have a shilling.
But you must make good use of your legs." The boy
was willing enough to earn the shilling, so he ran and
fetched the tinderbox, which he gave the soldier, and
—Yes, now it comes!

Outside the town a high gallows was erected, and
all round it stood soldiers, besides several hundred
thousand people. The King and Queen sat upon a
beautiful throne, and opposite to them the judges and
all the council.

The soldier stood already on the top of the ladder,
but when they were about to put the rope round his
neck, he said that the condemned were always given

one harmless wish before being punished. He wished
so much to smoke one pipe of tobacco, the last he
should get in this world.

This the King could not refuse, so the soldier took
out his tinderbox and struck fire. One—two—three,
and like a flash the three dogs stood before him, the
one with eyes like a teacup, that with eyes like a mill
wheel, and the one with eyes like the Round Tower
of Copenhagen.

"Help me now, that I may not be hanged," the
soldier said; and the dogs at once chased the judges
and the council, catching one by the legs and another
by the nose, and threw them up high in the air.

"You must not touch me," the King said, but the
biggest of the dogs caught hold of him as well as the
Queen, and threw them after the others. Then the
soldiers were frightened, and all the people cried.
"Good soldier, you shall be our king, and marry the
beautiful Princess."

They then seated him in the King's carriage and the
dogs sprang on in front, crying "Hurrah!" The boys
whistled with their fingers, and the soldiers presented
arms. The Princess came out of the brazen tower, and
was elected Queen, which pleased her well enough.
The marriage feast lasted a whole week, and the dogs
sat at the table with the others, making eyes at those
around them.

The Flax ℒ

T HE flax was in full bloom; it had pretty little blue flowers as delicate as the wings of a moth, or even more so. The sun shone, and the showers watered it; and this was just as good for the flax as it is for little children to be washed and then kissed by their mother. They look much prettier for it, and so did the flax.

"People say that I look very well," said the flax, "and that I am so fine and long that I shall make a beautiful piece of linen. How fortunate I am; it makes me so happy, it is such a pleasant thing to know that something can be made of me. How the sunshine cheers me, and how sweet and refreshing is the rain; I am so happy, no one in the world can feel happier than I am."

"Ah, yes, no doubt," said the fern, "but you do not know the world yet as well as I do, for my sticks are knotty"; and then it sung quite mournfully—

> "Snip, snap, snurre,
> Basse lurre;
> The song is ended."

"No, it is not ended," said the flax. "Tomorrow
the sun will shine or the rain fall. I feel that I am
growing. I feel that I am in full blossom. I am the
happiest of all creatures."

Well, one day some people came, who took hold
of the flax and pulled it up by the roots; this was
painful; then it was laid in water as if they meant to
drown it; and, after that, placed near a fire as if it
were to be roasted; all this was very shocking. "We
cannot expect to be happy always," said the flax; "by
feeling pain as well as good, we become wise." And
certainly there was plenty of evil in store for the flax.
It was steeped, and roasted, and broken, and combed;
indeed, it scarcely knew what was done to it. At last
it was put on the spinning wheel. "Whirr, whirr,"
went the wheel so fast that the flax could not think.
"Well, I have been very happy," he thought in the
midst of his pain, "and I must be contented with the
past"; and contented he was till he was put on the
loom, and became a beautiful piece of white linen.
All the flax, even to the last stalk, was used in making
this one piece. "Well, this is quite wonderful; I could
not have believed that I should be so fortunate. The
fern really was not wrong with its song of

'Snip, snap, snurre,
Basse lurre.'

But the song is not ended yet, I am sure; it is only just beginning. How wonderful it is that after all I have suffered, I am made something of at last; I am the luckiest person in the world—so strong and fine; and how white, and what a length! This is something different from being a mere plant and bearing flowers. Then, I had no attention, nor any water unless it rained; now, I am watched and taken care of. Every morning the maid turns me over, and I have a shower-bath from the watering-pot every evening. Yes, and the clergyman's wife noticed me and said I was the best piece of linen in the whole parish. I cannot be happier than I am now."

After some time the linen was taken into the house, placed under the scissors, and cut and torn into pieces, and then pricked with needles. This certainly was not pleasant; but at last it was made into twelve garments of that kind which people do not like to name, and yet everybody should wear one. "See, now then," said the flax; "I have become something of importance. This was the plan for me; it is quite a blessing. Now I shall be of some use in the world, as everyone ought to be; it is the only way to be happy. I am now divided into twelve pieces, and yet we are all one and the same in the whole dozen. It is such good fortune."

Years passed away; and at last the linen was so worn it could scarcely hold together. "It must end very soon," said the pieces to each other; "we would gladly have held together a little longer, but we must not expect what cannot be." And at length they fell into rags and tatters, and thought it was all over with them, for they were torn to shreds, and steeped in water, and made into a pulp, and dried, and they knew not what besides, till all at once they found themselves beautiful white paper. "Well, now, this is a surprise; a glorious surprise, too," said the paper. "I am now finer than ever and I shall be written upon, and who can tell what fine thing I may have written upon me. This is wonderful luck!" And sure enough the most beautiful stories and poetry were written upon it, and only once was there a blot, which was very fortunate. Then people heard the stories and poetry read and it made them wiser and better; for all that was written had a good and sensible meaning, and a great blessing was held in the words on this paper.

"I never imagined anything like this," said the paper, "when I was only a little blue flower, growing in the fields. How could I fancy that I should ever be the means of bringing knowledge and joy to men? I cannot understand it myself, and yet it is really so. Heaven knows that I have done nothing but what I was obliged to do, and yet I have been given one joy and honor after another. Each time I think that the song is ended; and then something higher and better begins for me. I suppose now I shall be sent on my travels about the world, so that people may read me. It must be, for I have more splendid thoughts written upon me than I had pretty flowers in olden times. I am happier than ever."

But the paper did not go on its travels; it was sent to the printer, and all the words written upon it were set up in type, to make a book, or rather, many hundreds of books; for so many more persons could have pleasure and profit from a printed book than from the written paper; and if the paper had been sent about the world, it would have been worn out before it had got half through its journey.

"This is certainly the wisest plan," said the written paper; "I really did not think of that. I shall stay at home, and be held in honor, like some old grandfather, as I really am to all these new books. They will do some good. I could not have wandered about as they do. Yet he who wrote all this has looked at me, as every word flowed from his pen upon my surface. I am the most honored of all."

Then the paper was tied in a bundle with other papers, and thrown into a tub that stood in the washhouse.

"After work, it is well to rest," said the paper, "and a very good chance to think. Now, for the first time, I can think of what is in me; and to know oneself

is true progress. What will be done with me now,
I wonder? No doubt I shall still go forward. I am
always going forward, as I know quite well."

Now it happened one day that all the paper in the
tub was taken out, and laid on the hearth to be burned.
People said it could not be sold at the shop, to wrap
up butter and sugar, because it had been written upon.
The children in the house stood round the stove; for
they wanted to see the paper burn, because it flamed
up so prettily, and afterwards, among the ashes, so
many red sparks could be seen running one after the
other, here and there as quick as the wind. They
called it "seeing the children come out of school," and
the last spark was "the schoolmaster." They often
thought the last spark had come; and one would cry,
"There goes the schoolmaster"; but the next moment
another spark would appear, shining so beautifully.
How they would like to know where the sparks all
went to! Perhaps we shall find out some day, but we
don't know now.

The whole bundle of paper had been placed on the
fire, and was soon alight. "Ugh," cried the paper as
it burst into a bright flame; "ugh." It was certainly
not very pleasant to be burning; but when the whole
was wrapped in flames, the flames mounted up into
the air higher than the flax had ever been able to raise
its little blue flower, and they glistened as the white
linen never could have glistened. All the written let-

ters became quite red in a moment and all the words and thoughts turned to fire.

"Now I am mounting straight up to the sun," said a voice in the flames; and it was as if a thousand voices echoed the words and the flames darted up through the chimney, and went out at the top. Then a number of tiny beings, as many in number as the flowers on the flax had been, and unseen to mortal eyes, floated above them. They were even lighter and more delicate than the flowers from which they were born; and as the flames went out, and nothing remained of the paper but black ashes, these little beings danced upon it; and whenever they touched it, bright red sparks appeared.

"The children are all out of school, and the schoolmaster was the last of all," said the children. It was good fun, and they sang over the dead ashes—

> "Snip, snap, snurre,
> Basse lurre;
> The song is ended."

But the little unseen beings said, "The song is never ended; the most beautiful is yet to come."

But the children could neither hear nor understand this, nor should they, for children must not know everything.

The Last Dream of the Old Oak

I N the forest, high up on the steep shore, and not far from the open seacoast, stood a very old oak tree. It was just three hundred and sixty-five years old, but that long time was to the tree as the same number of days might be to us; we wake by day and sleep by night, and then we have our dreams. It is not so with the tree; it must keep awake through three seasons of the year, and does not get any sleep till winter comes. Winter is its time for rest; its night after the long day of spring, summer, and fall. On many a warm summer, the flies that live for only a day had fluttered about the old oak, enjoyed life and felt happy; and if, for a moment, one of the tiny creatures rested on one of his large fresh leaves, the tree would always say, "Poor little creature, your whole life is only a single day! How very short. It must be quite sad."

"Sad! what do you mean?" the little creature would

257

always answer. "Everything around me is so wonderfully bright, and warm, and beautiful, that it makes me happy."

"But only for one day, and then it is all over."

"Over!" repeated the fly; "what is the meaning of all over? Are you all over too?"

"No; I shall very likely live for thousands of your days, and my day is whole seasons long; indeed, it is so long that you could never reckon it."

"No, then I don't understand you. You may have thousands of my days, but I have thousands of moments in which I can be merry and happy. Does all the beauty of the world stop when you die?"

"No," said the tree; "it will last much longer—longer than I can even think of."

"Well, then," said the little fly, "we have the same time to live; only we reckon differently." And the little creature danced and floated in the air, happy in her delicate wings of gauze and velvet, happy in the balmy breezes, laden with the fragrance of clover fields and wild roses, elder blossoms and honeysuckle, from the garden hedges, primroses, and mint, and the smell of all these was so strong that the perfume was almost too delightful for the little fly. The long and beautiful day had been so full of joy and sweet delights, that when the sun sank low it felt tired of all its happiness and enjoyment. Its wings could hold it up no longer, and gently and slowly it glided down upon the soft waving blades of grass, nodded its little head as well as it could nod, and slept peacefully and sweetly.

"Poor little fly!" said the oak; "what a terribly short life!" And so, on every summer day the dance was danced again, the same questions asked, and the same answers given. The same thing was kept up through many generations of tiny flies; all of them felt merry and happy.

The oak kept awake through the morning of spring, the noon of summer, and the evening of fall; its time of rest, its night, drew near—winter was coming. Already the storms were singing, "Good night, good night." Here fell a leaf and there fell a leaf. "We will rock you and lull you. Go to sleep, go to sleep. We will sing you to sleep, and shake you to sleep, and it will do your old twigs good; they will even crackle with pleasure. Sleep sweetly, sleep sweetly, it is your three-hundred-and-sixty-fifth night. But you are but a youngster in the world. Sleep sweetly, the clouds will drop snow upon you, which will be quite a coverlet, warm and sheltering to your feet. Sweet sleep to you, and pleasant dreams." And there stood the oak, stripped of all its leaves, left to rest during the whole of a long winter, and to dream many dreams in its life, as in the dreams of men. The great tree had once been small; indeed, in its cradle it had been an acorn. It was the largest and best tree in the forest. Its top

towered above all the other trees, and could be seen
far out at sea, so that it served as a landmark to the
sailors. It had no idea how many eyes looked eagerly
for it. In its topmost branches the wood pigeon built
her nest, and the cuckoo carried out his usual con-
certs, and his notes echoed amid the boughs; and in
fall, when the leaves looked like beaten copper plates,
the birds would come and rest upon the branches
before taking their flight across the sea. But now it
was winter, the tree stood leafless, so that everyone
could see how crooked and bent were the branches
that sprang from the trunk. Crows came by turns
and sat on them, and talked of the hard times which
were beginning, and how hard it was in winter to get
food.

It was just about holy Christmas time that the tree
dreamed a dream. The tree had a kind of feeling that
the happy time had come, and in his dream he fancied
he heard the bells ringing from all the churches round,
and yet it seemed to him to be a beautiful summer's
day, mild and warm. His great top was crowned
with spreading fresh green leaves; the sunbeams played
among the leaves and branches, and the air was full of
fragrance from the blossoms; painted butterflies chased
each other; the summer flies danced around him, as if
the world had been made merely for them to dance
and be merry in. All that had happened to the tree
during every year of his life seemed to pass before

him, as in a happy procession. These were wonderful and happy moments for the old tree, full of peace and joy; and yet, amidst all this happiness, the tree felt a wish that all the other trees, bushes, and flowers beneath him, might be able also to remember, as he had done, and to feel the same happiness. The grand, old oak could not be quite happy in the midst of his enjoyment, while all the rest, both great and small, were not with him. At length his wish was satisfied. Up through the clouds came the green tops of the trees, and the oak saw them rising, and growing higher and higher. Bush and herb shot upward, and some even tore themselves up by the roots to rise more quickly. The birch tree was the quickest of all. Every child of the wood, even to the brown and feathery rushes, grew with the rest, while the birds rose with the melody of song. On a blade of grass, that fluttered in the air like a long green ribbon, sat a grasshopper, cleaning his wings with his legs. May beetles hummed, the bees murmured, the birds sang, each in his own way; the air was filled with the sounds of song and gladness.

"But where is the little blue flower that grows by the water?" asked the oak, "and the purple bell-flower, and the daisy?" You see the oak wanted to have them all with him.

"Here we are, we are here," sounded in voice and song.

"But the beautiful thyme of last summer, where is that; and the lilies-of-the-valley, which last year covered the earth with their bloom; and the wild apple tree with its lovely blossoms; and all the glory of the wood, which has grown year after year?"

"We are here, we are here," sounded voices higher in the air, as if they had flown there beforehand.

"Why this is beautiful, too beautiful to believe," said the oak in a joyful tone. "I have them all here, both great and small; not one has been forgotten. Can such happiness be imagined?" It seemed almost impossible.

"In heaven with the Eternal God, it can be imagined, and it is possible," sounded the answer through the air.

And the old tree, as he still grew upwards and onwards, felt that his roots were loosening themselves from the earth.

"It is rightly so, it is best," said the tree, "no chains hold me now. I can fly up to the very highest point in light and glory. And all I love are with me, both small and great. All—all are here."

Such was the dream of the old oak; and while he dreamed, a mighty storm came rushing over land and sea, at the holy Christmas time. The sea rolled in great billows towards the shore. There was a cracking and crushing heard in the tree. The root was torn from the ground just at the moment when in his dream he fancied it was being loosened from the earth. He fell—his three hundred and sixty-five years were passed as the single day of the flies. On the morning of Christmas day, when the sun rose, the storm had ended. From all the churches sounded the joyful bells, and from every fireside, even of the smallest cottage, rose the smoke into the blue sky, like the smoke from the thank offerings on the Druids' altars. The sea became calm, and on board a great ship that had outridden the tempest during the night, all the flags were hung, as a token of joy and festivity. "The tree is down! The old oak—our landmark on the coast!" cried the sailors. "It must have fallen in the storm of last night. Who can replace it? Alas! no one." This was a funeral oration over the old tree; short, but heartfelt. There it lay stretched on the snow-covered shore, and over it sounded the notes of a song from the ship—a song of Christmas joy.

> "Sing aloud on this happy morn,
> All is fulfilled, for Christ is born;
> With songs of joy let us loudly sing,
> 'Hallelujahs to Christ our King.'"

Thus sounded the old Christmas carol, and everyone on board the ship thought happy thoughts, through the song and the prayer, even as the old tree had felt lifted up in its last, its beautiful dream on that Christmas morn.

The Blue Mountains &

THERE were once a Scotchman and an Englishman and an Irishman serving in the army together, who took it into their heads to run away on the first chance they could get. The chance came, and they took it. They went on traveling for two days through a great forest, without food or drink and without coming across a single house. Every night they had to climb up into the trees for fear of the wild beasts that were in the wood.

On the second morning the Scotchman saw from the top of his tree a great castle far away. He said to himself that he would certainly die if he stayed in the forest without anything to eat but the roots of grass, which would not keep him alive very long. As soon, then, as he got down out of the tree he set off toward the castle, without so much as telling the other two that he had seen it at all. He traveled on most of the day, so that it was quite late when he reached the castle and, to his great disappointment, found nothing but closed doors and no smoke rising from the chimneys. He thought there was nothing for it but to die, after all, and he had lain down beside the wall, when he heard a window being opened high above him. At this he looked up and saw the most beautiful woman he had ever set eyes on.

"Oh, it is fortune that has sent you to me!" he said.

"It is indeed," said she. "What are you in need of, or what has sent you here?"

Said he, "I am dying for want of food."

"Come inside, then," she said; "there is plenty here."

So he went in to where she was, and she opened a large room for him, where he saw a number of men lying asleep. She then set food before him, and after that showed him to the room where the others were. He lay down on one of the beds and fell sound asleep. And now we must go back to the two that he left behind him in the wood.

When nightfall and the time of the wild beasts came, the Englishman happened to climb up into the very same tree on which the Scotchman was when he got sight of the castle; and as soon as the day began to dawn and the Englishman looked to the four quarters of heaven, what did he see but the castle too! Off he went without saying a word to the Irishman, and everything happened to him just as it had done to the Scotchman.

The poor Irishman was now left all alone. He did not know where the others had gone to, so he just stayed where he was, very sad and miserable. When night came he climbed up into the same tree as the Englishman had done on the night before. As soon as day came he also saw the castle and set out toward it; but when he reached it he could see no signs of fire or living being about it. Before long, however, he heard the window opened above his head, looked up, and beheld the most beautiful woman he had ever seen. He asked if she would give him food and drink, and she answered kindly and heartily that she would if he would only come inside. This he did very willingly, and she set before him food and drink that he had never seen the like of before. In the room there was a bed, with diamond rings hanging at every loop of the curtains, and everything else that was in the room was so beautiful that he actually forgot that he was hungry. When she saw that he was not eating at all she asked him what he wanted yet. Said the Irishman, "I will neither eat nor drink until I know who you are, or where you came from, or who has put you here."

"I shall tell you," said she. "I am an enchanted princess, and my father has promised that the man who sets me free from the spell shall have the third of his kingdom while he is alive and the whole of it after he is dead, and marry me as well. If ever I saw a man who looked likely to do this, you are the one. I have been here for sixteen years now, and no one who ever came to the castle has asked me who I was except you. Every other man that has come, so long as I have been here, lies asleep in the big room down there."

"Tell me, then," said the Irishman, "what is the spell that has been laid on you and how you can be freed from it."

"There is a little room there," said the princess, "and if I could get a man to stay in it from ten o'clock till midnight for three nights I should be freed from the spell."

"I am the man for you, then," said he.

Then she brought him a pipe and tobacco, and he went into the room; but before long he heard a hammering and knocking on the outside of the door and was told to open it.

"I won't," he said.

The next moment the door came flying in, and those outside along with it. They knocked him down, and kicked him, and knelt on his body till it came to midnight; but as soon as the cock crew they all went away. The Irishman was little more than alive by this time. As soon as daylight appeared the princess came and found him lying full length on the floor, unable to speak a word. She took a bottle, rubbed him from head to foot with something from it, and then he was as sound as ever. But after what he had got that night he was very unwilling to try it a second time. But the princess urged him to stay, saying that the next night would not be so bad, and in the end he gave in and stayed.

When it was getting near midnight he heard them ordering him to open the door, and there were three of them for every one that there had been the evening before. He did not make the slightest movement to go out to them or to open the door, but before long they broke it up and were in on top of him. They laid hold of him and kept throwing him between them up to the ceiling or jumping above him until the cock crew, when they all went away. When day came the princess went to the room to see if he was still alive, and, taking the bottle, put it to his nose, which soon brought him to himself. The first thing he said then was: "I am a fool to go on getting myself killed for anyone I ever saw. I will be off and stay here no longer."

When the princess heard him say this she entreated him to stay, reminding him that one more night would free her from the spell. "Besides," she said, "if there is a single spark of life in you when the day comes, the stuff that is in this bottle will make you as sound as ever."

With all this the Irishman decided to stay: but that

night there were three at him for every one that was
there the two nights before, and it looked very un-
likely that he would be alive in the morning after all
that he got. When morning dawned and the princess
came to see if he was still alive, she found him lying
on the floor as if dead. She tried to see if there was
breath in him, but could not quite make it out. Then
she put her hand on his pulse and found a faint movement in it. So she poured what was in the bottle
on him, and before long he rose up on his feet and
was as well as ever he was. Well, that business
was finished, and the princess was freed from the
spell.

The princess then told the Irishman that she must
go away for a little while, but would come back
for him in a few days in a carriage drawn by four
gray horses. He told her to "be aisy" and not speak
like that to him. "I have paid dear for you for the
last three nights," he said, "if I have any share of you
now"; but in the twinkling of an eye she had gone.
He did not know what to do with himself when he
saw that she was gone, but before she went she had
given him a little rod, with which he could, when he
pleased, waken the men who were sleeping there.

After being thus left alone, he went in and stretched
himself on three chairs that were in the room, when
what does he see coming in at the door but a little
fair-haired boy!

"Where did you come from, my lad?" said the Irishman.

"I came to make ready your food for you," said he.

"Who told you to do that?" said the Irishman.

"My mistress," answered the lad—"the princess that was under the spell and is now free."

By this the Irishman knew that she had sent the lad to wait on him. The lad also told him that his mistress wished him to be ready next morning at nine o'clock, when she would come for him with the carriage, as she had promised. He was greatly pleased at this, and next morning, when the time was drawing near, went out into the garden. But the little fair-haired boy took a big pin out of his pocket and stuck it into the back of the Irishman's coat without his noticing it, and he fell sound asleep.

Before long the princess came with the carriage and four horses and asked the boy whether his master was awake. He said that he wasn't. "It is bad for him," said she, "when the night is not long enough for him to sleep. Tell him that if he doesn't meet me this time tomorrow it is not likely that he will ever see me again all his life."

As soon as she was gone the fair-haired boy took the pin out of his master's coat, who instantly awoke. The first word he said to the lad was: "Have you seen her?"

"Yes," said he, "and she told me to tell you that if you don't meet her at nine o'clock tomorrow you will never see her again."

He was very sorry when he heard this, and could not understand why the sleep should have fallen upon him just when she was coming. He decided, however, to go early to bed that night, in order to rise in time next morning, and so he did.

When it was getting near nine o'clock he went out to the garden to wait till she came, and the fair-haired boy along with him; but as soon as the boy got the chance he stuck the pin into his master's coat again, and he fell asleep as before.

Precisely at nine o'clock came the princess in the carriage with four horses and asked the boy if his master had got up yet; but he said: "No, he is asleep, just as he was yesterday."

"Dear! dear!" said the princess. "I am sorry for him. Was the sleep he had last night not enough for him? Tell him that he will never see me here again; here is a sword that you will give him in my name, and my blessing with it."

With this she went off, and as soon as she had gone the boy took the pin out of his master's coat. He awoke instantly, and the first word he said was: "Have you seen her?" The boy said that he had, and there was the sword she had left for him. The

Irishman was ready to kill the boy out of anger, but when he gave a glance over his shoulder the fair-haired boy was gone.

Being thus left all alone, he thought of going into the room where all the men were lying asleep, and there among the rest he found his two friends. Then he remembered what the princess had told him—that he had only to touch them with the rod she had given him and they would all awake; and the first he touched were his own friends. They started to their feet at once, and he gave them as much silver and gold as they could carry when they went away. There was plenty to do before he got all the others wakened, for the two doors of the castle were crowded with them all the day long.

He was so grieved at the loss of the princess that finally he thought he would go about the world to see if he could find anyone to give him news of her. So he took the best horse in the stable and set out. Three years he spent traveling through forests and wildernesses but could find no one able to tell him anything of the princess.

At last he fell into so great despair that he thought he would put an end to his own life, and to do this he laid hold of the sword that she had given him by the hands of the fair-haired boy. But on drawing it from its sheath he noticed that there was some writing on one side of the blade. He looked at this, and read

there: "You will find me in the Blue Mountains."
This made him take heart again, and he gave up the
idea of killing himself, thinking that he would go on
in hope of meeting someone who could tell him where
the Blue Mountains were.

After he had gone a long way, without thinking
where he was going, he saw at last a light far away
and made straight for it. On reaching it he found it
came from a little house. As soon as the man inside
heard the noise of the horse's feet he came out to see
who was there. Seeing a stranger on horseback, he
asked what brought him there and where he was going.

"I have lived here," said he, "for three hundred
years, and all that time I have not seen a single person
but yourself."

"I have been going about for the last three years,"
said the Irishman, "to see if I could find anyone who
can tell me where the Blue Mountains are."

"Come in," said the old man, "and stay with me
all night. I have a book that tells the history of the
world. I will go through it tonight, and if there is
such a place as the Blue Mountains in it we shall find
it out."

The Irishman stayed there all night, and as soon
as morning came rose to go. The old man said he
had not gone to sleep all night for going through the
book, but there was not a word about the Blue Mountains in it. "But I'll tell you what," he said: "if there

is such a place on earth at all, I have a brother who lives nine hundred miles from here, and he is sure to know where they are if anyone in this world does."

The Irishman answered that he could never go those nine hundred miles, for his horse was giving out already. "That doesn't matter," said the old man. "I can do better than that. I have only to blow my whistle, and you will be at my brother's house before nightfall."

So he blew his whistle, and the Irishman did not know where on earth he was until he found himself at the other old man's door, who also told him that it was three hundred years since he had seen anyone and asked him where he was going.

"I am going to see if I can find anyone that can tell me where the Blue Mountains are," he said.

"If you will stay with me tonight," said the old man, "I have a book of the history of the world, and I shall know where they are before daylight if there is such a place in it at all."

He stayed there all night, but there was not a word in the book about the Blue Mountains. Seeing that he was rather discouraged, the old man told him that he had a brother nine hundred miles away, and that if anyone could find out about them it would be he; "and I will help you," he said, "to reach the place where he lives before night." So he blew his whistle, and the Irishman landed at the brother's house before nightfall. When the old man saw him he said he had not seen a single man for three hundred years, and was very much surprised to see anyone come to him now.

"Where are you going?" he said.

"I am going about asking for the Blue Mountains," said the Irishman.

"The Blue Mountains?" said the old man.

"Yes," said the Irishman.

"I never heard the name before; but if there are any, I shall find them out. I am master of all the birds in the world, and I have only to blow my whistle and every one will come to me. I shall then ask each of them to tell where it came from, and if there is any way of finding out the Blue Mountains that is it."

So he blew his whistle, and when he blew it all the birds of the world began to gather. The old man questioned each of them as to where they had come from, but there was not one of them that had come from the Blue Mountains. After he had run over them all, however, he remembered a big eagle that was missing, and wondered that it had not come. Soon afterward he saw something big coming toward him, darkening the sky. It kept coming nearer and growing bigger, and what was this, after all, but the eagle! When she arrived the old man scolded her and asked what had kept her so long behind.

"I couldn't help it," she said. "I had more than

twenty times further to come than any bird that has come here today."

"Where have you come from, then?" said he.

"From the Blue Mountains," said she.

"Indeed!" said the old man; "and what are they doing there?"

"They are making ready this very day," said the eagle, "for the marriage of the daughter of the King of the Blue Mountains. For three years now she has refused to marry anyone, until she should give up all hope of the coming of the man who freed her from the spell. Now she can wait no longer, for three years is the time that she agreed with her father to wait without marrying."

The Irishman knew that it was for himself she had been waiting so long, but he had no hope of reaching the Blue Mountains all his life. The old man noticed how sad he grew, and asked the eagle what she would take for carrying this man on her back to the Blue Mountains.

"I must have sixty cattle killed," said she, "and cut up into quarters, and every time I look over my shoulder he must throw one of them into my mouth."

As soon as the Irishman and the old man heard that, they went out hunting, and before evening they had killed sixty cattle. They made quarters of them as the eagle told them, and then the old man asked her to lie down till they would get it all heaped up on her back. First of all they had to get a ladder of fourteen steps so they could get on the eagle's back, and there they piled up the meat as well as they could. Then the old man told the Irishman to mount, and to remember to throw a quarter of beef to her every time she looked round. He went up, and the old man gave the eagle the word to be off, and off she flew and every time she turned her head the Irishman threw a quarter of beef into her mouth.

As they came near the borders of the kingdom of the Blue Mountains, however, the beef was gone, and when the eagle looked over her shoulder what was the Irishman at but throwing a stone between her tail and her neck! At this she turned a complete somersault and threw the Irishman off into the sea, where he fell into the bay that was right in front of the king's palace. Fortunately the points of his toes just touched the bottom, and he managed to get ashore.

When he went up into the town all the streets were gleaming with light and the wedding of the princess was just about to begin. He went into the first house he came to, and this happened to be the house of the king's hen-keeper. He asked the old woman what was causing all the noise and light in the town.

"The princess," said she, "is going to be married tonight against her will, for she had been expecting every day that the man who freed her from the spell would come."

278 ANDERSEN'S FAIRY TALES

"There's a gold piece for you," said he. "Go and bring her here."

The old woman went, and soon came back along with the happy princess. She and the Irishman rushed into each other's arms, and were married, and had a great wedding that lasted for a year and a day.